CREEP AND CHASE

Also by Ruth Dowley

Hiding Places

CREEP AND CHASE

Ruth Dowley

VICTOR GOLLANCZ

LONDON

First published in Great Britain 1996
by Victor Gollancz
An imprint of the Cassell Group
Wellington House, 125 Strand, London WC2R 0BB

Text copyright © Ruth Dowley 1996

A catalogue record for this book is
available from the British Library

ISBN 0 575 06378 5

Typeset in Great Britain by Rowland Phototypesetting Ltd,
Bury St Edmunds, Suffolk
Printed in Great Britain by St Edmundsbury Press Ltd,
Bury St Edmunds, Suffolk

To Matthew and Neville

with love

Chapter 1

"Mum says the bin's got to be emptied, and it's your turn."

"It's not my turn!"

"It is."

"You liar." Peter grabbed Ben's arm.

"Let go. You're hurting me! I did it when you were at Christopher Cole's."

"I did it after that!" Peter got him into a half nelson.

"Ow-w!"

"*Ba*-by!"

Ben kicked backwards and whacked Peter's ankle. Peter tackled him to the floor. Ben started yelling.

The office door opened upstairs. Mum came down fast.

"What's going on?"

"He's killing me!" shouted Ben.

"Get off him, Peter!"

"He kicked me!"

"I just said it was his turn to empty the bin, and he attacked."

"Do we have to have this every time I ask you to do something? You know how busy I am! Get off THIS MINUTE!"

Peter let go, and Ben got up rubbing his arm. He pushed up his sleeve to examine a red patch.

Mum glared at Peter. "Why are you always getting at him?"

"He kicked me. You didn't see!"

"I'm sick of this quarrelling! SICK of it!"

She shoved a chair out of the way and seized the kettle. "We'll put up a list and you can each mark when you do a job. You empty the bin this time, Peter."

"It's not my *turn*!"

"I expect it is."

"It isn't. That's not fair. You always take his side."

"Come on, quickly, while I'm here." Water blasted into the kettle. Mum looked out of the cottage window and sighed. Now she was going to be in her martyr mood.

The phone started ringing in the office.

"Oh, *honestly*! That'll be the Computercrat aggroing now." She ran upstairs.

"I'll get you, slug!" Peter pushed past Ben and yanked the plastic bin liner. It was so full with squashed-down rubbish, it wouldn't budge. An orange-juice carton and a soup tin jumped out on to the floor.

"You pick that up," Peter demanded.

And then Ben did one of those things Peter could never really explain which he liked and disliked at the same time.

He said, "Oh, all right," and *did* pick up the carton and the tin. That was the good part.

But he did it as if it didn't matter a bit. That was the irritating part. He even held on to the bottom of the bin while Peter pulled out the sack, and then opened the door when he took it outside.

"Give me about an hour," Mum said upstairs and hung up the phone.

She called down, "If you're going to Jacob's, take the scraps."

"Shall we?" Ben asked.

Peter hesitated. No point wrecking the rest of the day. "Creep and Chase?"

"Wicked!" said Ben. He called, "Mum, we're taking them now."

Peter grabbed the bag of leftovers. They jogged across the back lawn. The football lay on the grass.

Peter shot for the goal. The ball rebounded off the post. Ben volleyed it.

The ball rocketed into the corner of the goal.

"Yes!" shouted Ben.

Clever git, thought Peter, turning away.

A high drystone wall bordered the back of the lawn. The top stones had fallen off long ago where Peter and Ben always climbed over. Now the wall was like a giant stile.

Peter lifted the carrier bag above his head to rest on a flat stone. He loved climbing the wall. Suddenly your head came clear and, as if a wand had been waved, like the opening shot of a film with the music rising, there it all was.

You could see the house with Devil's Loft behind on one side and Dark Den at the top of the orchard on the other. Beyond the yard a bit of the red tin roof over the Peak caught the sun. Then the fields, some dotted with arcs, stretched all the way down to the brook.

What you saw from the top of the wall was Jacob's farm—the most brilliant place on earth!

Chapter 2

Leo belted through the rough grass. No one got near Jacob's without Leo knowing. He had turned up at the farm, half-grown and hungry, four years ago. He hadn't been claimed, so of course Jacob adopted him.

He stood on his hind legs against the wall where Peter wanted to get down.

"Move it, monster," Peter told him.

Leo just went on swinging his great raggedy tail. Peter had to leave the scrap bag and use both hands to reach down and prise away the big paws.

He lost his balance and had to leap for it. When he was on the ground, Leo stood over him licking his face and hair.

"You're drowning me, slobber-jobber!" Peter blocked the wet tongue with an elbow, but he was sorry when Leo left off and jumped up against the wall again. He'd heard Ben coming.

"Leo lion!" Ben leaned down and scratched behind Leo's ears where he liked it.

"Hand us the bag," said Peter, getting up.

Ben swung it over Leo's head and looked towards the drive. "Jacob's not here. The Land Rover's gone."

"Bags dens then," said Peter. He dropped the scraps. "Your

turn to carry." He ran off down the slope towards the farm-house, calling Leo. But Leo stayed with Ben.

"Wait!" shouted Ben. He slid down the wall. "You'll see the grousers first! Stop, or it's not fair."

He dived for the carrier. Leo kept jumping in front of him, wanting to be fussed.

They raced after Peter to the drive and round the side of the house. Ben dumped the scraps by the back porch. Peter was already going into the farmyard.

"Stop now!" yelled Ben.

Too late. Peter looked left and saw through the orchard gate that the grousers were up between Dark Den and the Bog.

"I bag Devil's Loft," he shouted.

"That's not fair."

Peter sprinted down the farmyard to the tractor shed to get the flag. Leo and Ben caught up with him as he came out tossing and catching it. The three of them put on a spurt to the Peak.

A lot of the straw had gone in the winter, but the Peak was still high. They scrambled up the prickly bale steps and ran along the top. They always planted the flag right at the end.

Peter jabbed it between two bales. The flag was a red T-shirt. The shirt had been Peter's and then Ben's.

Mum said Peter was lucky always getting clothes first. Peter thought that wasn't worth a thing compared to the baby-waby treatment Ben got for being younger.

"What shall we play for?" asked Ben.

"Whoever wins has to do the washing-up tonight."

You won by either getting back to your den with the flag

11

or capturing the other person's den and bopping him when he came in.

"No way. It's your turn to wash up."

"OK then, whoever wins does two nights in a row." Peter flashed Ben a smile. "No argy-bargy."

"Sound. You're on."

Peter sat on the edge of the stack to take the quick way down. "Yow!"

He dropped on to the loose straw below, his knees folding under him.

"Yow-ow!" Ben dropped beside him and rolled on to his back.

Leo's face appeared over the edge of the Peak. He whined. He always climbed the stack when they did and then felt cheated when they jumped. It was too steep a jump even for a big dog.

"Brainless beast," Peter called. He was cross with Leo for waiting for Ben at the wall.

Out of the corner of his eye, he saw Ben look across to the bottom of Devil's Loft. The death slide was fixed to the old hoist in the open loading bay at this end.

He's checking that the bar's in place, he thought. He thinks I'll use it for Creep and Chase.

The death slide was fab. You held on to the bar and leaped out of Devil's Loft like a kamikaze. You zizzed through the air so fast, you left your guts behind.

Jacob had fixed the bottom of the wire to an iron frame which used to have a swing in it. You got your balance when you hit the ground by running through the frame before you let go.

OK. Let him think I'll go that way, thought Peter. He purposely looked up at the bar under the pulley. He saw Ben pretend not to notice.

Ben jumped up and ran along the side of the Peak. He whistled. Leo turned back and lolloped down the bale steps swinging his tail. He never held a grudge.

He tried to stuff his head between Ben's legs.

"Now we'll have to shut him in the porch, and Jacob's not here. Poor lion."

"Oh, let him stay loose," said Peter, giving Ben another false clue. If he'd been planning to do any creeping, he wouldn't want Leo loose as he was a dead give-away. But he knew he was safe. Ben wouldn't want Leo roaming about either.

"No chance," Ben said. "I've got enough handicaps with the grousers, thanks to you."

They took Leo back to the farmhouse. Ben went with him into the porch, gave him a quick pat, nipped out and shut the door.

Leo looked through the window, hurt. His tail drooped between his legs.

"Sorry, boy." Ben scratched the glass. "We'll throw sticks for you after."

He heard Leo whining as he climbed over the gate into the orchard. He felt really mean, but now he had to concentrate on tactics.

The grousers were chomping grass on the edge of the Bog. Their heads popped up like a gaggle of glove puppets. As soon as he landed, the gander raised his wings.

They would make a terrible racket if he went the orchard way to get the flag. Peter would know Dark Den was unprotected. Well, perhaps he could use that.

13

Opposite the orchard gate on the other side of the farmyard, Peter went up the outside stone steps to Devil's Loft.

After the Peak was rebuilt at harvest, any extra straw went in this end of the Loft. Then he and Ben made a camp high up among the rafters. They even used to keep supplies in a space behind some loose stones at the top of the back wall.

Now it was spring, the straw store was empty apart from the tea chests they sat on when it rained.

Peter stood on the top step outside Devil's Loft and held up his arm for the exchange of signals. He could see over the orchard gate to Dark Den. Ben waited outside, looking across to the Loft.

Ben raised his arm. Peter's arm moved side to side. Ben's arm moved side to side. Both arms dropped.

Start!

Chapter 3

Peter dived into Devil's Loft and slammed the door. He must make Ben think he was in a hurry. Then Ben would hare off to beat him to the Peak. But Peter would be capturing Dark Den.

He'd kill himself laughing when Ben came back with the flag, and it was all for nothing. He'd kill himself laughing when Ben had to do the washing-up two nights in a row, no argy-bargy.

He better just be sure Ben didn't come across the farmyard and try to capture Devil's Loft. He needed something to block the door. He hurriedly piled the tea chests against it, but they weren't heavy enough.

There was a grey, cobwebby storage room between this end of Devil's Loft and the bit over the tractor shed where the death slide was. They called it the Spook Room. Peter ran in.

Ghosty shapes of ancient horse collars, rotting harnesses, rope, trug baskets and old tools lay about under grey dust. He and Ben never hung about in here because the light was so dim, but it was fun to run through fast, imagining a demon or a ghoulie in transparent clothes on your heels.

Near the Spook Room door, someone had saved a rusty

pitchfork. Like a devil's pitchfork. Maybe that had given them the idea for the name of the Loft, but it was so long ago, Peter couldn't remember. They'd played here for ever.

The pitchfork might be just what he needed. He dragged it back to the outside door.

Shoving the tea chests aside, he used the fork as a prop. Its prongs dug into the wooden floor and the handle jammed firmly under the middle door strut. Perfect!

Now he had to be quick. He raced through the Spook Room into the part of the Loft over the tractor shed.

He stuck his head halfway out of the open loading bay and glanced quickly at the Peak over near the bottom of the orchard.

No sign of Ben yet.

He was tempted to leap out quickly on the death slide. But that would wreck his plan. Instead, he lowered himself through the trapdoor in the floor.

He scrambled down the ladder and did a fast tiptoe through the shed. He peeped out.

A sparrow flew from under the eaves to peck in the farmyard. A hen was having a dust bath in a tractor rut in the sun. Must be all clear.

The tractor stood near by with the trailer hitched up ready for the evening rounds. He scooted to its cover and steadied himself against the seat as he crept past.

The touch of the warm metal flung up a memory of when he was little. Jacob used to lift him and sit him there to pretend to drive. Then he'd have to get down so Ben could have a turn.

He made a break for the top of the farmyard, up the side of the big barn. He flattened against the corner near the orchard gate.

Listen. Sorted! Ben must have gone through the orchard to the Peak. The grousers were all over the shop, honking their heads off.

He was just about to leave the shelter of the barn and climb over the gate, when he saw a blur of colour whizz through the slit of sight he had of the grass by Dark Den.

Little sneak! Ben had outguessed him. He'd stirred up the geese on purpose and come straight back. He was *expecting* an attack.

Dark Den was an old stable without windows. They ducked in and out of the bottom half of the stable door, so it was really difficult to see when you first went in. Ben would have zapped him for trespassing for sure.

Peter shot out of view. OK, clever dick, he thought. If you're going to guard Dark Den, *I'll* capture the flag.

He tore back down the farmyard and out. He was travelling so fast by the time he got to the top of the Peak that he didn't watch where he was treading. His foot plunged into a space where four bales cornered and brought him down.

He rubbed his ankle crossly. He mustn't lose time. He stood up. The ankle wanted longer to recover, but he forced it to take his weight.

He limped to the end and grabbed the flag. He better not risk the jump though. He went down Leo's way.

But it was OK. When he crept back into the farmyard, everything was quiet. He ducked into the tractor shed and climbed the ladder, smiling to himself.

He'd got the little prat now. Mummy's boy. He wasn't so smart when the odds were even.

As he came through the Spook Room, he could see nothing

had been disturbed. The pitchfork jammed the outside door shut, just as he'd left it.

Laughing out loud, he ran and pushed the handle aside. The heavy fork hit the floorboards with a thump.

He threw open the door, whirling the flag in a triumphant red circle.

"I've got it!" he shouted. "Bad luck, Benbo! Washing-up time!"

Leo joined in with a bark from inside the porch.

Peter cupped his hands round his mouth and yelled really loudly towards Dark Den. "I've won, I've won!"

"Oh, no, you haven't!"

Ben danced out from behind the tea chests and tagged him. "Fooled you! I crept up the ladder while you were on the Peak. I've taken Devil's Loft. *I've* won."

Peter stepped backwards and scowled. "You haven't won. I'm on the step. I was in my den without being bopped."

"Don't try it on."

"You didn't tag me while I was in there."

"You were in the doorway."

"Sorry, you weren't quick enough, dumbo. Doorways don't count."

"Cheat!"

Peter wrestled him on to the outside stairway. "Take that back, fat face, or I'll shred you!"

He straddled Ben's waist and pinned him down. "Have I won or have I won?"

The stone steps dug into Ben's back. He strained to keep his neck from hanging over the edge. "Get off! You can make me say you've won, but it won't mean anything."

It made Peter sizzle when Ben was logical about him being stronger. He felt like shoving him down on to the bit of concrete where the trailer backed to unload straw.

Leo barked and crashed against the porch door. They heard wheels scrunch on the drive. Jacob was back!

Chapter 4

Jacob had been shopping. They helped him carry the bags from the Land Rover.

"Here's a warm welcome then." He always said that when they went into the kitchen because it was so cosy with the Aga, and the red and blue patterned rug and Jacob's armchair with cushions squashed over the worn bits.

But they knew he also meant it was a warm welcome because they were there. He was always glad to see them.

"We brought some scraps," said Peter. He wished he'd carried them all the way. Then he could have said, I brought some scraps.

"Now that's kind. You'll be in favour at teatime."

Jacob opened the deep drawer in his desk and took out the metal strongbox he kept under the pig-breeding records. "I'll just pop my bit of cash in with the valuables."

He unlocked the strongbox and tucked a few ten-pound notes beside the legal papers. Then they put away the food in the larder. At last only a white paper bag lay on the wooden table.

"Wait till you see what I've got." Jacob opened the end of the bag.

A sweet buttery smell seeped into the kitchen. He eased out a treacle tart, criss-crossed with frills of succulent pastry.

The three of them stared at it longingly.

"I think it's still warm," said Ben, leaning his face close and sniffing.

"Stop it, Ben!" ordered Peter.

"I don't reckon I can wait for supper, do you?" said Jacob.

"I know I couldn't," agreed Ben.

"What do you say we test a bit?"

"Yes, please!"

Peter thought Mum wouldn't want them to eat Jacob's tart. He'd probably bought it to last him several days. But when Jacob got a sharp bone-handled knife and sliced through the pastry, Peter thought he'd faint with hunger.

Jacob put his kettle on the Aga ready to make tea and then lifted out enormous pieces of tart on to three plates.

They pulled up chairs and ate with their hands. No one said a thing until they were pressing up the last crumbs.

"Well, that was scrumptious," said Jacob. "That Ted at the bakery's a wonder."

"I'll say." Ben sucked a finger noisily.

"Have a bit more, my duck."

"Yes please." Ben held out his plate, grinning.

"Greedy guts!" accused Peter. "That's Jacob's supper."

"Oh, yes. No thanks. I've had enough really."

Jacob put another piece on Ben's plate anyway. "It'll never be as good as this moment," he said. "You'll have some more too, now, Peter."

Peter was horrified to see how much they'd eaten already, but why should Ben have more and not him?

"Just a tiny piece."

"That's my boy."

Peter liked it when Jacob said things like that. He was always on your side. Why couldn't Mum be like Jacob? And Dad. Jacob wouldn't have gone to Africa to work on their stupid computers.

Mum did her computer programming from home, but when the company Dad was working for went bankrupt, the only place he could get a contract was in Sudan. He was going to be there five more months. It was terrible.

"Dad said to say hello. It was on the e-mail yesterday."

"What's this e-mail then?"

"You know, electronic mail. He types a message on his computer in Khartoum and sends it through the telephone wires, and we can call it up on our screen in the cottage."

"Well, I reckon that's a real service. Keeps you feeling linked together. Will you say hello from me? And say I wish he could be back for harvest."

Both Mum and Dad sometimes helped on the farm. They said it kept them from going square-eyed and radioactive from the PC screens.

But Mum hadn't had much time to spare since Dad went away, what with her job and looking after them and the house. She got really crabby when she was indoors all day.

Peter didn't enjoy the second piece of tart as much as the first. There was hardly any left now.

Jacob didn't seem to mind. He moved to his old armchair by the Aga and sat drinking his tea, smiling at them. Jacob's smile happened in every part of his face. Even the lines in his forehead curved upwards.

It's all right really, thought Peter, because he likes giving us things. But he wished there was something really good he could give Jacob. Just him, not dimwit Ben.

Chapter 5

"Coming to do the rounds?" asked Jacob.

As they went out, Leo jumped up from his guard position in the porch. He slept in his basket there at night with the door open, unless the weather was bad.

"Shall we bring the scraps?" asked Ben.

"That's the ticket."

All Jacob's land sloped gently down to the brook. Here and there the fields were scattered with the rounded corrugated roofs of arc shelters for the pigs.

The pigs moved about with Jacob's crop rotation. "My best workers," Jacob called them. "Champion ploughers and fertilizers in one."

Jacob backed up the tractor and filled the open feed container on the trailer. He grew most of the pigs' food—a lot of barley and some wheat. A machine ground all the ingredients.

Jacob swung over a couple of bales from the Peak in case any of the arcs needed a top-up. His arm muscles were as strong as iron.

"Now what did I do with that toolbox?" He always had his tools at the ready.

"Were you working on the new weaner arc?" asked Peter.

Jacob had part-time help from the village, but Dad usually gave a hand making the pig shelters.

"I was. Good thinking! Must have left it in the shed."

"Want me to fetch it?" asked Ben, but Peter had already shot off with Leo at his heels.

He ran to the welding shed under Devil's Loft.

Sure enough, the toolbox lay beside the base-frame of an extra-big arc. A group of weaner pigs would live in it when they left their mothers at eight weeks.

Peter shifted a piece of corrugated iron out of the way. It wobbled in the air, sounding like distant thunder.

Leo whined and ran off. He hated noises like that. Jacob thought it must be because of something that happened to him when he was a puppy.

Peter grabbed the toolbox and dashed back. He hopped on the trailer beside Ben.

They bumped down to the home field where some sows had just farrowed. The sows often had their piglets overnight, but sometimes they were lucky and saw them born.

Peter was always amazed how easily the little bodies would slide from the stretched vulva below the sow's anus. Any part could appear first, a head, a tail, legs. Often within a second, out came the whole piglet. It lay there slippery and shiny-wet, its body limp like it was asleep.

Then really quickly it was alert and moving, its eyes opening, a perfect miniature pig. It was usually on its way to find a drink before the birth cord broke three or four minutes later.

"How do they know which way to go?" Peter asked Jacob once.

"Perhaps they follow the direction of the sow's hair growth, perhaps they smell the milk," said Jacob. "Some way, nature's got it all organized as usual."

Inside the hedge, the home field was divided into two paddocks with electric wire on posts that were easy to move. The pigs quickly learned to keep away from the wire.

The tractor and trailer stopped in the service corridor between the paddocks.

A sow looked up from the water trough. It was easy to see she was suckling a new litter. Her teats made a prominent pink row beneath the pale skin of the rest of her body.

"Hello then, my lovely," Jacob said.

He stood a second or two, smiling and watching her. He aimed to look over each of the animals every day.

He switched off at the "electric gate" in the fence. A special handpiece retracted the wires into a coil while they took the food through.

Ben ran ahead and squatted to look in the nearest arc. Leo went with him, but then trotted on down the field with his nose to the ground.

Half the front of the arc was boarded. Around the entrance, a low fender filled with straw let the tiny pigs come out in the air without getting lost. The mother could step over.

Ben peeped into the snug tunnel home. The sow lay stretched out in the cosy nest she'd made from chopped straw. Ten babies lined up against her, some sucking, some dozing off.

When Ben stroked her head, she grunted contentedly. The sows liked to be scratched behind the ears the same as Leo.

He picked up one of the babies and held it against him. He loved their tiny trotters and their little pink bodies, all warm with velvety white hairs still soft on them.

Peter stood on the trailer, filling up feed buckets.

"Are you going to *help?*" he shouted.

Ben gently put the piglet back in the nest and ran over. He took a bucket.

After farrowing, the mothers got room service beside their arcs. Soon they were all out, bright-eyed and curly-tailed, tucking in.

"Now where's your pig chocolate-Milk Tray?"

That's what Jacob called the vegetable peelings, fruit cores and stale baked goods they saved. The scraps didn't go far, but that wasn't the idea. Jacob said a bit of variety perked anyone up a treat.

They went along the arcs handing out nibbles while Jacob checked the piglets.

Peter looked past a conker tree in the next field down to where the lane crossed the brook. The water splashed up at the ford, and a sports car shot out.

"Looks like Nick's car on the lane," he called, "but it can't be, can it?" Nick only came on the last Friday in the month.

The growl of a powerful engine carried over the fields and, in a moment, the screech of tyres on the curve. They knew then that it was Nick after all.

"He's burning some rubber!" Ben said.

"This *is* an honour," said Jacob, but you could tell he was really chuffed. "I better pop back to the house."

He whistled and Leo galloped up the field.

Ben patted him. "Pwaw!"

"What?" asked Peter.

"Take a whiff!"

Peter sniffed. "You've rolled in poop! Disgusting animal. The pigs wouldn't do that."

Sometimes the pigs lay in mud wallows to keep cool. They needed to because pigs have hardly any sweat glands. But they never lay in manure and were really particular about dumping away from their sleeping places.

They left the trailer ready to move on to the other paddocks and went back on foot. A snowy blackthorn was in blossom by the hedge gate. Bees hummed in and out and a little holly blue butterfly flew past.

"Listen," said Jacob. A two-note bird call came from further along. "That's the chiffchaff back from his winter travels."

Nick met them at the top of the farmyard. He saw himself as a smooth dresser. In his tailor-cut tweed jacket and cap, he couldn't have looked more different from Jacob, coming up in his baggy boiler suit. Of course, Nick was much younger too.

"Hello, brother," Nick said with a grin.

He's on the scrounge, thought Peter.

"*Hel*-lo then!" said Jacob. He clapped a hand on Nick's shoulder. "How are you?"

"Great," said Nick. He nodded at the boys. "Hi."

Nick hardly ever spoke to Peter and Ben. Mum thought it was because Jacob always spoiled him when he was growing up, and he was jealous of them taking his place. "He hasn't grown up *yet* if you ask me," she said.

"We saw you from the home field," said Jacob. "I've got some fine new litters down there just now."

"You're a glutton for hard work. Don't know why you haven't got them all under cover in efficient units. Randall's made a packet of money with his."

28

"What d'you mean hard work? I don't muck out or transport slurry, and the pigs are as healthy and full of beans as any animal can be. I love to see them."

Nick smirked, but then stopped himself and said, "Look, I need to talk to you." He shifted his eyes to Ben and Peter.

He must want to wheedle something big if he's got to get rid of us, thought Peter. It made him mad the way Nick was always sponging off Jacob.

This winter he'd asked for a bit of straw because he'd run short and then came and cleaned out Devil's Loft. Dad said he hadn't paid a penny for it.

"Come and have a cup of tea." Jacob's big smile took in first the boys, then Nick. "I've got a piece of treacle tart we can recommend."

Peter looked at Ben. "Let's throw sticks for the stinky lion."

Chapter 6

They opened the orchard gate and let Leo through. The grousers were grazing on the far side of Dark Den and decided not to notice.

The Bog stretched the length of the back of the big barn. Between the barn and the pond grew a thicket of bushes and brambles. The brambles were as lethal as coiled barbed wire. Wrens flitted in and out to nests which hung in the thorny stalks like lost balls, but people had to go right round to get to the bottom of the orchard.

They looked for sticks. Leo knew what was coming and got into turbo position, head low, rear in the air ready for take off.

"I know!" said Peter. "Make him go in the Bog. Get rid of the pong."

"Yes!" exclaimed Ben.

Leo wasn't dead keen to fetch from the Bog. It was named for its squelchy bottom, and in the summer a forest of plants grew under the surface.

"Get him going. Catch!"

Leo loved trying to intercept their catches. He barked and leaped left, then right, as the stick whizzed from Peter to Ben, Ben to Peter.

Suddenly, Peter launched it sideways into the Bog.

Leo galloped to the edge. He skidded to a stop. He tested the water with one paw and came back sheepishly.

He tried to stuff his head between Peter's legs.

"Oh, pathetic! Get in there, you mangy mutt!"

"It's probably cold," said Ben.

"What do you think his hair's for?"

"If I were on the other side, and we were throwing across, he might get in."

"You can't get round," said Peter, but, at the same time, he had a picture of Ben trying and falling in. Mum wouldn't like it. Ben would be in trouble.

"I might be able to get along from the Peak end," said Ben, studying the opposite bank.

"No chance."

"I'll try, shall I?"

"Bet you can't."

Leo followed Ben down the orchard, but couldn't go with him along the far bank. He whined.

Ben jumped over a clump of kingcups on the muddy rim. A startled toad hopped from under the leaves.

"Whoops!" exclaimed Ben.

Leo yapped and the toad plopped into the Bog.

Ben eased along the edge, clinging to branches. He had to keep stopping to unhook brambles from his jeans and sweat-shirt.

Halfway up, an alder tree leaned over the water. He hitched a leg round the trunk for balance and freed his hands.

"This'll do," he yelled. "Call him and start throwing."

Peter waved a stick. Leo bounded up the orchard.

31

After a couple of splashdowns, they judged the distance and sent some brilliant catches across. Ben waved the bait on his side urging Leo to come and get it. Peter shouted Fetch.

Leo just wagged his tail and ran up and down the side of the pond.

"It's useless! He won't," Peter called. He threw half-heartedly a last time.

Ben reached out to catch. The heel of his trainer slid over the bent grass on the edge of the bank. He clutched the tree with his anchor foot, but his legs splayed apart.

"Help!" he screamed, grabbing the trunk hand behind shoulder as one leg hovered over the water.

"Nice one, Benbo!" yelled Peter.

Ben's new position suddenly got Leo interested. He waded in and doggy-paddled across the Bog.

Ben struggled to unwrap one leg from the tree without plunging the other into the water, but Leo arrived first. He tried to climb out on top of him. He was masses too big. There was no room.

"Call him! He's going to pull me in!"

Peter doubled up, hooting. Ben was for it now.

Shouting came from near the farmhouse. Leo growled, turned with a splash and swam back frantically.

Ben, muddy and splattered, got himself up. He scrambled along the bank, getting his hands scratched as he tried to hurry. He ran up the orchard.

Jacob and Nick stood by the porch. Nick was having a major tantrum. His face and neck were blotched red with yelling.

Leo barked and pawed at the orchard gate. Peter let him through, but blocked Ben's way.

Leo raced to Jacob and pushed his head into his boiler suit. He shook himself, spraying both men.

"Get *away!*" bellowed Nick.

Jacob tried to stroke Leo, but he was too anxious to keep still. He paced around, whining.

"You know I can't give the bank a personal guarantee on a loan that size," Jacob said to Nick. "If it were called in, I'd have to sell part of the farm."

Peter could see he was trying to talk calmly, but Nick shouted back at him.

"I've told you, it *won't be called in!*" He stamped his foot. "I'm going through a rough patch, and I'm asking my brother to help me out, that's all."

"You know I want to help all I can. That's why I've gone on with the money every month, even though we're square."

"You're expecting that back."

"Not until you're able. We've kept it informal."

"You pretend to be generous, but when it comes to the crunch, you're as mean as they come."

"Nick, Nick. There's always a home here for you, and Pam too, if things come to the worst."

"I wouldn't come back and live with you if my life depended on it. Miser!"

"You're asking me to put the farm at risk."

"You're putting me at risk. Stuff the farm. I hope you do lose it!"

The definite way he said that sent a chill through Peter. *Could* anything happen to the farm?

"Nick—"

"You'll regret this—I'm telling you!"

Nick turned and ploughed into Leo. He kicked out at him savagely. Leo yelped. Nick stormed off to his car.

Jacob bent and hugged Leo's dripping body. He ran his big hands along his back while Leo trembled and whimpered. "There now. Good fellow."

They heard the sports car wheel-spin out of the drive.

"I *hate* Nick!" said Peter.

Ben pushed past him and ran to the farmhouse.

Jacob went on soothing Leo. "He's not himself. Not himself," he murmured. "He wouldn't really want to hurt an animal."

Peter could see it wasn't only Leo Nick had hurt. It was Jacob.

Chapter 7

They finished the feeding rounds with Jacob and went home for supper. Ben still claimed he'd won Creep and Chase.

Mum wouldn't listen to anything about the game and snapped, "Stop quarrelling! You know it's your turn to wash up, Peter. I've put the list on the fridge for you to mark when you've done a job."

"If you're going to cheat, I won't *play* Creep and Chase any more," said Ben.

They both went quiet. Neither of them wanted that.

Then Ben said, "Oh, all right. We'll call it a draw if you like."

Peter agreed by not answering, but he hated the way it seemed as if Ben were being generous. He always got one up somehow.

On top of that, the next morning, Saturday, a postcard from Dad dropped through the letterbox. It was to Ben.

Peter followed Ben when he went upstairs to show Mum. It had a picture of some Africans taking their goats to graze. Peter saw that the first sentence said, "Remind you of us moving the pigs?"

Mum was rummaging around the office irritably. "I've lost

35

a blue folder. I had it yesterday. The Computercrat will fuse his chips if he has to give me those figures again."

The Computercrat was her boss. Mum said he wanted ordinary work done by yesterday and his pet projects by the week before he'd thought of them.

"You haven't been in here moving things, have you?"

"No," said Ben, all innocence.

"Peter?"

"No."

"Are you sure? Weren't you playing a computer game last night?"

"I DIDN'T MOVE ANYTHING!" Why was he the one she always suspected?

"Don't shout!"

"Don't accuse me of things then!" Peter scanned the room. "Have you used the phone?"

"Yes."

He lifted the phone book.

Mum pounced on a folder beneath.

"*There* it is! Thanks." She took it to the PC. No apology for blaming him.

"Mum, look." Ben showed her the card. She put her arm around him while they read it. Peter wandered away.

"Do you want to see, Peter?" Mum asked, but he stayed by the door. "I expect you'll get yours tomorrow. You know what the post's like."

"He probably didn't send me one."

"Of course he did. I expect he wanted to write to you separately since he sends the e-mail to all of us." She opened the blue folder and typed something on the PC keyboard.

She doesn't care, thought Peter. Her little darling's got what he wants.

"I'll have to go and see to the washing in a minute if you two want to play that CD-ROM game Christopher Cole lent you."

"Want to?" asked Ben.

"No, it isn't much cop."

"It's better with two. Go on."

"I don't *want* to!" Peter went into his and Ben's bedroom. He'd left the game on his shelf.

"WHERE IS IT?"

Ben ran in and pulled out Chris's disk from under the bottom bunk.

"Who said you could touch it?" demanded Peter.

"I was only checking out the cover."

"He lent it me, not you!" He snatched the game and viced Ben's shoulder. "Don't touch my things without permission!"

"Ow!"

"What's going on now?" Mum called.

"Peter won't let me look at Chris's game."

"Don't be selfish, Peter!" She came in. "Chris wouldn't mind Ben using it."

"He would. He knows he wrecks everything."

"I don't!"

"You do, dickhead."

"Oh, leave him if he's like that, Ben," said Mum. "Want to use Dad's golf disk? I'll see if I can find it."

They went into the office together.

Peter thumped stiff-legged down the stairs and outside. It

37

always turned out *something* was his fault. It always ended up with Ben getting fussed over.

Leo met him by the wall, but kept looking back for Ben.

"Even you like him better than me," Peter told him.

Leo licked his hands, not owning up.

Coming over the wall, Peter had seen the tractor down in the fields, so he sat on the top step outside Devil's Loft to wait. Leo spread his big body over three steps and rested his head on Peter's trainers, panting and drooling.

"Slobber-soak," complained Peter, but he didn't push him off.

When Jacob drove into the farmyard, he stared at Peter for a second. He switched off the engine and came over.

"Hello, my duck. Funny thing. For a moment, you took me back to Nick when he was young. He used to play in that loft."

Peter didn't want to remind Jacob of Nick. Jacob was thinking about Nick because Nick had been horrible.

"How are things today?" asked Jacob. He patted Leo who was bumping against his legs.

"All right."

"Ben not here?"

Peter shook his head.

"No Creep and Chase then. I envy you. I was so much older than Nick, we never played together. It's more fun with two."

That was almost the same as what Ben had just said about the computer game. Peter looked away.

"I'm off to take some gilts to Whittlesford. William Head's bought them to mate with his boars. How about keeping me company? I'd appreciate a hand with the loading."

Peter jumped up. "Yeah!"

"Run and ask Mum then. Shall we ask Ben to come too? But he may not be about. You see."

Peter knew he'd have to ask Ben, because Mum would know Jacob wouldn't leave him out. Ben horned in on everything.

He wished Ben would drop off a cliff.

Chapter 8

On the way to the gilts' paddock, Peter walked by himself in front of Ben and Jacob, not speaking.

As he came to the gate, he heard an odd noise. He hesitated, then climbed over.

"What's that?" asked Ben, coming up. "Sounds like snoring. Cripes, somebody's crashed out in the field!"

"Shush!" demanded Peter.

He listened and looked about. Nobody was in sight. He bent under the hedge. The noise was terrific.

Jacob and Ben came quietly through the gateway. Jacob put down his bucket of pig meal.

Peter beckoned.

They walked over and peered behind some newly opened cuckoo pints. In a hollow of dry leaves lay the speckled body of a fast-asleep hedgehog.

"What a snorter!" whispered Ben. "He's even louder than Dad! Imagine that racket coming from someone the size of a brush head."

Jacob met Peter's eyes and smiled. "He's not long out of hibernation. Expect he was busy along the animal highway last night, stocking up." Jacob called the hedges animal highways.

40

"Good thing we've left Leo in charge at the house. He might be getting prickles up his nose."

He gave Peter the bucket.

He'd put a trailer in the gilts' paddock early that morning and given them their breakfast inside. The pigs were happy to follow Peter back in for more.

Jacob and Ben walked slowly behind with outstretched arms, but nobody bolted. Peter tipped out the meal on the straw, and Jacob fastened the tailgate.

Peter couldn't help cheering up as they drove off. It was great jiggeting about on the bench seat of the Land Rover, seeing so much more than you could in a car. The sun was climbing higher in the sky every day, coaxing, not just hedgehogs, but every living thing to wake up from its winter rest.

Jacob had a quick recce of the ploughed field next to the lane as they cruised down to the ford.

"Look!" he exclaimed. "First shoots are up! You do those wonderful things with computers, but it all depends on this."

They drove through the village and out on to the Whittlesford Road. Three miles along, they passed Nick's stables.

Two years ago, Nick had put up a new stable block. The place looked really impressive now.

"We could have stopped," said Jacob, meaning if Nick hadn't been angry with him.

He slowed for a moment while they watched graceful, long-legged horses grazing. Nick trained failed racehorses as hunters. Then they were worth a lot of money.

"Beauties, aren't they?"

Peter saw him search for any sign of Nick. He was glad he

wasn't about. Yesterday had made Nick threatening. He felt somehow Jacob needed to be protected from him.

Jacob sighed and speeded up.

Jacob and Nick's father, who was known for doing things in his own special way, had left them half the farm each—literally half each, with a line drawn on the plan through the centre hall-way of the farmhouse, the farmyard, down the fields to the brook.

Nick owned everything on the left side of the line and Jacob owned everything on the right.

But Nick was only interested in horses. Nick and Jacob had inherited this smallholding on the Whittlesford Road as well. Nick wanted to turn it into a proper stables.

Jacob had sorted it by buying Nick's share of the farm. It had cost him all his savings and monthly payments for six years, plus his share of the smallholding.

At William Head's they backed the trailer into a paddock and unloaded the gilts. Jacob quietly had a look in the water trough and the arcs. He was careful about where his animals went.

As they drove back, a shiny new Range Rover pulled out of Nick's place behind them. The driver began flashing his head-lights.

Jacob pulled off the road, and the Range Rover stopped in front.

"I think it's Ed Randall," he said. The Randalls owned the huge farm next to Jacob's, but they didn't mix much in the village.

Ed rolled down his window and called back, "Would you stop in on the way by? I'd like a word."

"Right you are," said Jacob.

Ben beamed at Peter. That meant they would go too. Although they'd heard plenty of rumours about it, they'd never been to the Randalls' farm.

42

Chapter 9

Ed Randall's combines, trucks and tractors were all the latest models and the biggest in the district. He even had a helicopter to spray his crops. It wasn't surprising they felt excited when Jacob's old Land Rover turned into the Randalls' drive.

Enormous fields without boundaries stretched away on both sides as far as you could see.

"It's like a prairie," said Peter.

Jacob nodded. "Nature pays a big price for this kind of farming."

The stone farmhouse and farm buildings had been converted into flats and holiday lets. The Randalls' long bungalow further down the drive was new.

Ed was talking to Mrs Randall through an open window. She closed it and disappeared as they pulled up.

Ed swaggered across and shook hands with Jacob. "Come into the house," he said. "See you've got some help along. You lads go and have a walk round, but don't fly off in the chopper!"

"All right, my dears?" asked Jacob.

"Yes, thanks!" said Ben. "Brill!"

They hurried down the tarmac drive to the new farm buildings. The first thing they saw was the helicopter perched on a transporter-truck like a giant insect. It had E. RANDALL stamped in big letters on both sides. All Ed Randall's farm equipment had his name printed on it.

"Wow!" said Ben. "I wish Jacob had a helicopter."

"Don't be a berk. You need hundreds of acres to have one. And anyway, Jacob says the wind can blow the chemicals all over the village. That's why he never puts any pigs in that field below the wood. It doesn't get much shelter."

Peter felt small against the huge windowless sheds and giant hoppers. Nothing grew near the buildings. A matted brown strip along the sides looked like grass zapped with weed-killer.

"It doesn't seem like a farm," he said.

"Come on. Let's go and see the animals," said Ben.

They slid back the door of one of the big buildings.

It was like going into Dark Den. They could hardly see a thing. But there was something in there because they could hear shuffling and squeals.

"There's a power cut," said Ben.

"No, listen. Electric fans."

Fans or not, the air was stuffy and thick with a stink of urine and manure. Gradually in the faint light from the ventilation shafts, they saw pens on each side of a central walkway.

"What's going on?" gasped Ben.

Crammed together in each pen were about thirty young pigs, perhaps three months old. They had just enough room to stand up.

"What are they doing in here? They don't get any exercise or fresh air. They can't even *see*!"

"I suppose it's an intensive unit," said Peter. He never

dreamed they were like this. "Wait a minute. There must be a light switch somewhere."

He felt round by the door and clicked on a row of central lights. Then they saw that pen after packed pen stretched down each side of the vast shed.

The pigs were nervous and squashed even closer together towards the back when Ben and Peter leaned over to look at them. Some climbed on top of each other. A rasping cough came from one buried underneath.

"They haven't got any straw," said Ben. "There's no separate place to dump."

"The pee and poop go through those slats in the floor," said Peter. But it didn't all go through because the pigs were smeared with dung.

"There's nowhere to be cosy, nowhere to play. It's cruel! Doesn't Ed Randall know how clever pigs are? They can scent as well as Leo."

"He doesn't even feed them himself. Look, the food's dropped out of that dispenser overhead."

All down the aisle, pigs were jostling and scrimmaging in the pens. Now and then one of them screeched.

"They're biting each other's ears and tails," said Peter. "No, not tails. Cripes, they've had their tails sliced off!"

Ben didn't want to see any more. "Let's go."

They opened the door into sun and lively air. The contrast was so strong, they couldn't help looking back. The shadowy pens looked like metal bins. Bins of living animals.

"Leave the light on for them," Ben said.

"Too right! I feel like just letting them out."

"But where would they go?"

45

They walked on, numb, hardly able to take in what they'd seen.

They came to a narrower shed. There was dim light inside this one, but what it showed them was even more terrible.

Sows were pinned down between metal bars which were so close to their bodies that they couldn't turn around or even walk forwards and backwards. Between the cages were small bare areas with warming lights where piglets were supposed to lie away from their mothers.

"Gees!" Ben swallowed. "Some of them are waiting to have babies. They'll hardly be able to move while they're farrowing."

"It's like the torture cages you see in castle dungeons," said Peter.

The mothers gave birth on a cold metal floor punched with drainage holes. There was no bedding.

"It must drive them mad not being able to make their nests," said Ben. "How long do you think they're kept like this?"

"Weeks if it's before they farrow till the babies are weaned. Look. These ones have got nasty sore places where they've rubbed against the bars."

Ben walked down the aisle, looking into the unhappy eyes of the sows. Many of the pigs lay on their sides without hope. One pawed again and again at her cage. Another one gnawed the bar in front of her. She'd cut herself doing it, and blood mixed with bits of froth on the edge of her mouth.

He wanted to stroke her, but he was afraid he'd touch a hurt place. He thought he might cry. He went quickly past Peter, and outside.

Peter closed his fist over a bar and yanked with all his might. He wished he had Jacob's muscles times a million. He wanted to pull the cages apart. He wanted to let the pigs out in a field and then smash the bars with a sledgehammer so they could never, never be used again.

They went and sat in the Land Rover, not looking at each other. Ben fought his tears. Peter felt as if a firework were ready to go off inside him.

Jacob wasn't long coming out of the house. Ed Randall followed him and leaned on the sill of the driver's door after Jacob got in. Peter glowered at him, but Ed was concentrating on Jacob.

"I'm offering you a good price," he said in a pushy voice.

Jacob started the engine. "I appreciate that, Ed, but I need all the land."

"Let's hope your brother pays his debts then. Bye for now." He straightened up and walked away.

Peter saw Jacob's eyebrows move in a question. Was Nick involved with Ed Randall? And what had it got to do with Jacob? What had it got to do with Jacob's *land*?

"He wanted to buy that field below the wood," said Jacob as they drove off, "but I don't reckon we'll sell, will we?" He smiled at Peter and Ben, then saw their faces. "What is it, my ducks?"

Peter exploded. "Don't sell him a centimetre! He should have his farm confiscated. He's not a farmer. He's a stinking torturer!"

"It was horrible, Jacob," said Ben. "He's got pigs jammed in cages. It's like doing it to Leo. Why don't the RSPCA stop him?"

"It's not just him, my love. I expect you saw farrowing crates. A lot of farmers use them. The idea is to stop the sows lying on the piglets."

"But that doesn't happen very much."

"You know it happens sometimes, and these sows have been bred and raised against nature. That can make them more clumsy."

"We saw how they're raised," said Peter fiercely. "Packed together in the dark. He thinks he's growing mushrooms!"

"You've got it right, my love. They're thought of as food, not animals."

"If people knew, they wouldn't buy that sort of food."

"It's easy not to think about what's behind it when you just have to rip open a bit of shrinkwrap and pop the meat in the oven."

"He's cut their tails off!"

"Being squashed together causes biting. A gnawed tail can lead to worse injuries. Some farmers cut off the testicles too."

"Oowah! Do they get painkillers?"

"Not usually if they're young." Jacob shook his head sadly.

"Can't we rescue them and take them to your place?" pleaded Ben.

"The law says they're his and allows what he does to them."

"How can it?" gasped Ben.

"Stuff the law then," said Peter. "Let's steal them!"

"He's probably got five thousand animals in those units."

"*Thousand!*"

"I don't think he's being consciously heartless. He just clicks off part of himself. We're all apt to do that you know, when something seems to get in the way of our interests. He'd probably tell you the pigs don't mind, because they've never known anything else."

"But they still have all their instincts. Bet he'd wish he knew something else if he'd been made to grow up like that!"

Peter tensed his fingers and bit pieces off the sides of his nails as they drove home. He'd always thought laws prevented cruelty to animals, that if you found someone being cruel, they would be made to stop.

Were laws only for some animals, sometimes? Didn't animals have any *rights*?

Chapter 10

When they got home, they rushed up to the office and told Mum.

"Can you tell what sort of farm meat comes from?" asked Peter. "You know, like eggs say 'free range'."

"I've seen an 'outdoor reared' label."

"Right! Don't buy anything made of pig unless it says 'outdoor reared' on it!"

"Don't buy anything made of *any* animal locked up inside," Ben said.

"OK, but if the meat's more expensive, I'll have to buy less. You can stock up with beans on toast. That's as good a protein."

"*Everyone*'s got to stop buying torture meat!" said Peter through clenched teeth.

"I'm telling everybody at school," Ben said.

Peter hammered on the wall. "That's not enough!"

"Stop it. You'll have the plaster down," said Mum.

"I'm thinking what to *do*! Could I write to the paper?"

"I don't see why not."

"Sound! I'm letting Ed Randall have it! Can I use the PC?"

"You can. Now." She pressed Close for the computer file she was working on and stood up.

"Look at that sun! I'm going over to the farm. I promised Jacob I'd scrub out the hen drinkers and put some new straw in the nesting boxes. If the Crat rings, tell him I've exercised my basic animal right to get outside."

"Want me to help?" asked Ben.

Peter frowned. Typical. Now they'd go off and leave him.

"If you like," said Mum.

"I was going to collect the eggs for Jacob anyway," said Ben.

Creep, thought Peter. Oh, let them do their little jobbies together. He didn't care. He was going to help the pigs.

He turned his back and sat down at the keyboard. When he was finished with him, Ed Randall was going to wish he were in a pork pie.

He jabbed the keys. Dear Sir.

He banged out how farmers like Ed Randall treated animals as if they were flesh-producing robots, how people who bought their meat were just as bad. But after a couple of paragraphs, he stopped.

For one thing, he realized that up until today he'd been just as much to blame as anybody else. For another, the way he was writing reminded him of getting told off.

When someone laid into you with don't do this, don't do that, you thought, I will if I want to. Get your nose out. The last thing you did was think of what you'd done from someone else's point of view. From a pig's point of view, for instance.

Nothing would change unless people saw it from a pig's point of view. He pressed Delete and held down his finger till he'd wiped the screen.

He closed his eyes. What would a pig on Ed Randall's farm say?

As he began to hear the pig, Peter felt as if a black hole were opening inside of him. Slowly, he started to write.

Dear Sir,

I was born a prisoner and have spent my entire life in prison. I don't know why I was sentenced.

My mother wanted to look after me, but she couldn't. She was trapped in metal bars. She couldn't even turn around while I was being born.

I found my way underneath the cage to feed. I lay on a hard floor like she did. Then I had to move away from her, because I was cold. I wanted to snuggle in a cosy protected nest and go to sleep, but my brothers and sisters and I had to lie in a bare place directly under a light bulb.

Two men came with a sharp knife and held me upside down. They cut off parts of my body. I lay in pain for a long time.

Since then I've lived in a small dark cell with many others. We can't move without bumping. There's nothing to make into a bed. There's nothing to do but stand up or lie down. Our feet get sore.

We try to go to the toilet in one area, but there are too many of us. The air in our cell stinks. We stand over the pit which collects our urine and dung. The dung sticks to our skin before dropping through the holes in the floor.

We're getting fatter, so there's less room all the time. We shove and bite each other to get more space and because we're bored. Sometimes the bites make me bleed.

Now the prison door is opening. We're being pushed towards a big truck. It's strange to walk so many steps at

once. I squeal and scream because I'm afraid. How long will
I travel in that big machine? Will I have water and food?

Perhaps at the end of the journey, I'll know at last why I
was sentenced.

Yours faithfully,

A. Pig

as dictated to Peter Tompkins.

He was running the spell-check when Mum came back. She
was humming to herself. She loved pottering about the farm.

"One of the geese is sitting on eggs," she told him.

"I know."

She laughed. "You don't miss much, do you?" She gave him
the *Whittlesford Echo* for the address.

"Well, you've stuck at it. Ready to run off a copy?"

She squatted and looked at what he'd written.

She went quiet. "Reading this is awful after being at Jacob's."

She touched his head. "You've convinced me. No more
factory-farm food in this house. Shall we e-mail a copy to Dad?"

Chapter 11

Before Dad picked up his e-mail on the work computer in Sudan on Monday, Peter got a postcard. The postmark was too faint to tell if it had been posted at the same time as Ben's.

It had a picture of some African farmers putting stones close to seedlings to help trap water near the roots. It said, "Imagine farming somewhere this dry—every drop of water precious! I miss our cool green fields almost as much as the games of footers with you + Ben."

Peter didn't show it to Ben. Dad hadn't said anything about *you + Peter* in Ben's card. Peter's name hadn't been mentioned in Ben's card.

But when they came home from school, Mum called down that Peter had a message waiting on the PC.

"Move it," he told Ben, and got in front when Mum called the e-mail on to the screen.

Dad had done an Internet search on intensive farming.

"Hey, prison pork is definitely off the menu! And crated calf and caged chicken. Ashamed of myself for not thinking about it properly before. I've surfed the Net. Intensive units are all over the place now—Africa to Asia."

"That's stinking," said Ben, looking over Mum's shoulder.

The message went on, "The locals in poorer countries often can't afford to eat the meat. Many Africans would be glad to have the regular supply of grain fed to battery hens."

"What a *fowl*-up," said Peter.

"You can bet someone's making money out of it," Mum said.

"Anyway, found an ally for you. Compassion in World Farming. E-mail address: tmobrien@ciwf.win-uk.net."

"Can we contact them, Mum?" asked Peter.

"All right."

"Can I help?" Ben asked.

"No way. You'd end up contacting the North Pole."

"I would not!"

"Leave him alone, Peter."

"OK, OK."

Peter changed the screen for sending a message. Ben watched for a minute and then drifted off into their room to do his homework.

Peter typed in the address. He described Ed Randall's pig-rearing and asked the Compassion people what they thought. He clicked Send.

When Mum had finished her programming, he logged back in. Someone called Tim had replied straight away.

They were really glad to hear from him. They said they were working for friendly environments for all farm animals. Peter felt chuffed because one of the suggestions they made was to write to a newspaper.

He was so excited the day the *Whittlesford Echo* came out, he looked at the clock about every five minutes. When the *Echo* finally poked through the cottage letterbox in the evening, he dived at it.

He knelt on the floor and whipped to the letters page. He coasted down the columns with his finger. The letter wasn't there.

Mum said it would probably be in the next week, but she was wrong. There was nothing again.

"That rotten editor," said Ben. "He thinks pigs are too lowly to count."

"Yeah," said Peter.

But privately he was afraid the letter hadn't been printed because he hadn't written it well enough. He'd let the pigs down. They were helpless. They had to just go on with their miserable lives day after day.

He was going to talk to Jacob about the letter getting ditched. He went to look for him in the farmhouse. Before he got to the kitchen, he heard him on the phone.

"Hello, Nick? I've been trying to get you. How are things going?"

There was a pause while Jacob listened.

"Nick, you haven't thought through what you're asking. Please calm down. Why have I had it? What do you mean? Hello?"

Nick must have hung up.

Peter went back outside. Why was Nick still making it sound as if Jacob was in trouble? The lousy sneak was up to something.

Peter knew it for sure when Nick didn't come on the last Friday that month.

Jacob had cider cooling in the larder, the same as always. It was the one tradition they'd kept after Nick moved to the smallholding and started living with Pam.

Nick always used to turn up about seven o'clock. Lately, he'd only stay for a ten-minute drink. Jacob would follow him out with boxes of eggs, saying things like "Why don't you and Pam come and have a meal with me sometime?" and "You take care now."

One Saturday though, Peter and Ben saw Nick. They'd been playing Creep and Chase.

Ben had Devil's Loft that time and Peter had Dark Den. After the start signal, they both decided to race straight for the Peak. There was fifty pence of next week's pocket money on a win.

Ben dashed through the Spook Room to the death slide. He grabbed the bar.

There was always a split second for Ben when he was afraid to jump. He'd never told Peter, but the first time they'd tried out the slide, even with Jacob standing underneath, he'd been so scared he almost wet himself.

Now he knew it was quite safe, so he would just take one steadying breath, look down at the old iron swing frame to orientate himself, and push off.

Then it was really fantastic, swishing through space like you were a parachutist, or a high-wire performer or an abseiler careering down a mountain.

Using the slide, he got to the Peak first, but when he'd jumped off the end with the flag, Peter came tearing full steam out of the bottom of the orchard.

Ben dodged back behind the bales, hoping Peter would climb the Peak and give him time to make a break for it.

Peter saw him.

"Not quick enough, Benbo!" he shouted. He stationed himself at the farmyard entrance, blocking the way back to Devil's Loft.

Ben crept round the other side of the Peak. Perhaps he could sneak up the orchard way.

But Peter was as alert as a fox. As soon as Ben left cover, he spotted him. He whooped and started chasing.

Ben hared round the Bog. In a straight race, he had no hope. Peter was a faster runner. But the grousers were near this end. If he could get them between him and Peter, he might make it.

He charged towards them, hoping to zip past and leave them to scatter, blocking Peter's way.

The goslings had hatched, and the grousers were extra stroppy. They raised their wings and began to hiss. Led by the gander, *they* decided to charge. Eyes narrowed, necks and heads stretched forward like bayonets, they rushed him.

"Yikes!" he screamed.

He swerved towards the blossoming apple trees. Just in time, he hoisted himself on to a forked branch above the angry army.

Peter stopped. "Run into a bit of trouble, Benbo?" he taunted.

Ben climbed through a carnival of pink buds, white flowers and insects giddy with nectar. But below him, the geese surrounded the trunk. They honked that he should come down instantly and be pecked.

Peter kept his distance till they found some of their favourite goose grass at the foot of the tree. As they plucked it, he spotted a gap. He streaked forward and sprang into the branches.

"Here comes a hole in your pocket!"

Beaks shot up, wings flapped. The grousers strutted about, honking and cackling at the new outrage.

Ben didn't dare drop to the ground. He went on up, but soon ran out of higher forks. He shinned backwards on to a branch.

Peter kept climbing.

"I'd say you were out on a limb, Benbo. Don't think it'll hold both of us." He straddled the branch, laughing, ready to try it anyway.

Ben started laughing too. "All right, stop, *stop*! I'm not bananas enough to get a broken neck for fifty pee."

Peter leaned out and bopped him.

It was then that they both heard horse's hoofs.

They looked through the apple blossom, past Dark Den and over the gate which led from the orchard directly into the drive. Nick came round the curve at the top mounted on one of his beautiful thoroughbreds.

As soon as he was in sight of the house, he reined in. He turned the horse without another look and trotted back up to the lane.

"Why did he do that?" asked Ben. "He can see Jacob's here because of the Land Rover."

Why ride all that way from Whittlesford and then change his mind about coming in?

"Shall we tell Jacob?"

"No, it'd cut him up," said Peter.

But he didn't like it. He wished he knew what was going on.

Chapter 12

The piglets in the home field didn't need fenders in front of the arcs any more. They played games with their straw, rooting and tossing it like the older pigs, but mostly they trotted after their mothers and scampered about the paddock.

Jacob called little pigs the original creep and chasers. They would squeeze into the creep where they could get special extra food, and then, after eating, they would rush out and belt after each other. They'd gallop and nudge like puppies.

When the piglets were this age, Peter and Ben used to play dead. They would lie completely still, and the piglets would dare each other to sneak up and investigate.

Eventually, there would be six or seven twitching their little snouts as they sniffed them all over. They couldn't resist. Jacob said pigs are the most curious creatures he knows.

But now Peter kept thinking how Ed Randall's piglets wouldn't ever run or play. They wouldn't even know if it was winter or summer.

It made him boil. The Compassion people said he should write to his MP and European MP.

He'd got slimy answers back from both of them. Sounded

like they hadn't even read what he said. They'd probably put his letter straight in the bin like the newspaper did.

One evening, weeks after he'd written, he saw the *Whittlesford Echo* plop on to the mat in the hall. He picked it up and flicked hopelessly through to the middle.

His eyes suddenly shot into focus. There, printed out word for word, being read all over the district, was the letter from A. Pig as dictated to Peter Tompkins.

He ran through the cottage.

"Mum!"

Ben saw the paper. "Is it in?"

Peter nodded.

"Yes!" shouted Ben.

"Well done," said Mum. "Want to tell Dad on the e-mail?"

Peter hadn't let Ben see the letter before he'd sent it. He left him reading it out loud to Mum while she scrubbed carrots.

When he came back downstairs, Ben was sitting rolling a ball from hand to hand on the kitchen table. The newspaper was folded open in front of him.

He cupped his hands round the ball and looked at Peter.

"You know the end of the letter where the pig's going to find out he's existed just so he can get killed and eaten by humans? It's just hit me. It's cold-blooded murder. I mean we don't need to do it, do we? Not like a wild animal eating for survival."

"That's why we have to make sure they have a good life like Jacob's pigs."

"But I don't want to murder Jacob's pigs either. I know they only travel as far as the slaughterhouse in Whittlesford, but what happens there? I bet they don't get coaxed in to be killed with

61

someone holding a bucket of meal in front of them. I bet they *know*."

"Do you want to give up bacon then?"

"But it's slices of flesh. Slices of creep and chasers."

"Are you going *vegetarian*?"

"I might be."

Peter liked the idea of the letter having a big effect on Ben, but the thought of him not eating meat at all narked him. It felt like he was going to pull another one-up.

"Mum, you won't try to make me vegetarian if he is, will you?"

"People have to make up their own minds about something like that," said Mum.

"Yeah, but you eat hardly any meat because of the fat. You might not want to buy stuff just for me."

"Don't be silly. I'm on a winner. No scrapping over the last piece, or the size if I cut it in half."

After supper, Peter took the letter over to show Jacob. He was on his way to the poultry house. The hens and geese put themselves to bed well before dusk. Jacob went and shut the door against foxes when he'd finished the evening rounds.

He leaned against the tractor and read the letter. "Poor creatures," he said. "I reckon you've done them a good turn."

"But it won't help the ones over at Ed Randall's, will it?"

"Not very likely, my duck. But letters like this might help there to be less like them in the future. That's what you've got to aim for."

"I'm getting some leaflets. Dad got me the address of Compassion in World Farming on the Internet. They're sending them."

"He did that from Africa? These computer link-ups are a marvel."

"The leaflets have got pictures of the farrowing crates. That'll help people imagine them better, won't it?"

"It will."

"But will it make any *difference*?"

"A few years ago it was legal to keep sows chained up in narrow stalls so they couldn't turn around all their lives. A big petition was organized by people like your Compassion friends. Now tethering's being banned in this country."

"Really? That's terrific!"

"Still not in a lot of other countries though. Something to write to the Euro MP about."

"I did write to both MPs, but they aren't going to bother."

"They are when they think enough people care."

"It takes so long. I wish it would all change *this minute*!"

"You just got to keep at it."

They walked on down the yard together. A late long ray of sun caught the blue sheen on the wings of some swallows skimming over the barn. Jacob's big smile filled his face.

"Look, there's another link-up for you. They came from Africa all under their own know-how and wing power."

"When?"

"Few weeks ago. The death's head hawkmoths do the same. Think of a little moth coming all that way. They're part of nature's Internet. In the air, through the seas, across the ground, she connects us all up on the big world ball. She's a wonder."

Chapter 13

The Computercrat was hassling Mum again. She had to keep in with him. Dad hadn't got any work yet for when he finished his contract in Sudan.

"I bet the Crat doesn't shop, cook, do the laundry and clean the house in between perfecting his precious computer packages!" she ranted.

She got herself wound up and crabbed about everything she could think of all through supper. "There's more mud on the stairs. I told you to leave your trainers by the back door."

"Sorry," said Ben.

"And I asked you to tidy your room. It's a heave!"

"I've cleaned up my things."

"No you haven't, goody-goody," said Peter. "Your maths charts are all over the floor."

"Since when?"

"Since you left them by the window and they got blown."

"Oh, thanks a mountain. You could have picked them up for me."

"Why should I? You can pick them up with the snotty tissues you left under the bed."

"I haven't left any."

"You have, slug."

"At least I don't drop smelly underpants and socks on *other* people's beds."

"At least I don't snoop through other people's private things and leave the tops off felt-tip pens and—"

"STOP IT!" shouted Mum. "I've got a splitting headache, and I've still got to finish that program tonight. Do something without making a fuss for once, Peter!" She bristled off up to the office.

Ben started to leave too.

"Where do you think you're going?" demanded Peter. "It's your turn to wash up."

"Mum did it yesterday, and I did it the day before."

"You did not!"

"Look at the list then." They'd tried marking the list on the fridge when they did a job, but they forgot so often that they argued as much as ever about whose turn it was.

Peter looked. "You cheat, Ben! You marked when you didn't do it." He nipped into the doorway. "You can just get on with it, snake."

"I'm not. I did it last. Ask Mum."

"She doesn't remember." He pushed Ben back into the kitchen.

"You can stop me leaving, but I'm not doing it."

"You ARE!"

Peter shoved him towards the sink. Ben tried to stand his ground. Peter rammed him. Ben fell against the table and caught a glass with his elbow.

The glass sped to the floor and smashed. It was one of the good ones.

Mum rampaged back downstairs.

"Sorry," wailed Ben. "He pushed me."

"He cheated! He's marked for washing-up when he hasn't done it!"

"I haven't!"

"I'm FED UP with you, Peter!" Mum yelled. "You're always looking out for yourself!"

Then the phone rang. It was Dad. The first thing Mum said was that Peter was getting at Ben again.

Peter went into the bedroom and wouldn't talk when it was his turn. And he wanted to. Dad hardly ever rang because e-mail was cheaper, but wasn't nearly as good as hearing someone's voice.

He could have told him about the petition he was going to take round the village to ask the government to ban farrowing crates. It was so unfair of Mum to say he was always looking out for himself when he was trying to help the pigs. And he hadn't meant the stupid glass to break anyway.

He climbed up on his bunk. He chewed the side of a thumb-nail while he listened to creep Ben describe some babyish vegetarian project he'd chosen at school. Slimeball. He spoiled everything.

Afterwards Mum came to find him. "You're a very silly boy. Dad was sad not to talk to you."

Peter turned the pages of a book he had on his bed and didn't look at her.

Mum sighed. "You'd better stay up here now while I clear up that broken glass." She'd changed from her Spitfire voice to her martyr one.

After about half an hour, Peter tiptoed out on to the landing.

The television was on downstairs. He'd have to wash up or he'd get yelled at again, but at least he could do it without anyone watching.

Mum's bedroom door was slightly open. She was sitting on the bed with her back to him. She was holding a photo of her and Dad she kept on the chest of drawers. She kept putting up a hand to wipe her face.

She was crying.

He suddenly knew she missed Dad as much as he did.

His stomach tightened into a nasty knot. He wanted to run in. He wondered whether if he said he was sorry, she would feel better. But he couldn't go in and admit he'd seen her crying. It would be embarrassing.

Ben could. She would have hugged Ben, and he would have made her feel better. He was her baby-waby. If Ben hadn't been born, she might have loved him like that.

He crept down to the kitchen, but somebody had already washed up.

Chapter 14

One Friday evening, Jacob drove over to a farm on the Whittlesford Road to arrange about the combine harvester for this year. Because he only had part-time help, he used to hire a combine and driver each summer.

During harvest, Dad or Mum often drove the tip-up trailer into the field alongside the combine. It unloaded without stopping harvesting.

Sometimes Ben and Peter climbed on the trailer at the gate. They'd lie back staring into sky, making their hands and feet disappear in the cool, running grains.

This year though Dad wouldn't be here, and Mum would probably be too busy to help. Jacob was hiring someone extra from the other farm.

"But cheer up," Jacob said. "It won't be long before I'll be teaching you two to drive the tractor and putting you on the holiday payroll."

"Yes!" said Ben. "Oh, blast. Peter'll be able to drive *ages* before me! It's jammy being oldest."

Peter thought that was a joke, but it was satisfying to imagine himself cruising round the fields with Ben having to watch from the gate.

That Friday, Christopher Cole and a friend of Ben's came to supper. They ended up with a great game of football. After the other boys had to go home, Peter and Ben went on taking turns shooting and being goalie.

They heard Leo start barking. A car coasted down the farm drive.

"Who's that?" said Peter.

They scrambled up the wall and looked over. The grass on the other side was long now and bright with red flags of poppies.

Nick's sports car stood empty on the drive, facing towards the lane. The door had been left open.

"That was a bit quiet for him," said Peter. "Not one engine rev. Anyway, the skunk's really missed Jacob this time."

Leo paced about by the front door, barking like mad.

"What's Leo doing?" asked Ben. Only sales reps ever used the front door. Everyone who knew Jacob went round the back.

Peter jumped down and started through the grass. Leo gave the house another bark, then galloped up to meet him.

The front door opened. Nick stood there with something tucked under his arm.

Peter knelt and grabbed Leo's collar. He was afraid he might make Nick lose his temper and get kicked again. Leo growled and strained.

Nick started to come out, but stopped when he heard what they all did—the sound of the Land Rover turning into the drive.

Nick rushed back through the farmhouse, leaving the door wide open. Peter could see right down the centre hallway. Nick ran to the back door, shoved a key in to unlock it and dashed out. Peter watched him go through the porch and into the farmyard.

Jacob stopped the Land Rover nose to nose with the sports car. Leo broke away from Peter and tore over, barking as if he had desperate news.

Ben jumped off the wall, and he and Peter ran to Jacob as well.

"Nick's in the yard," called Peter.

"Is he looking for me?"

"I don't know." Peter didn't like to say that Nick had actually legged it when he heard him coming.

But Jacob must have sensed awkwardness in his voice. He hesitated by the Land Rover for a moment, stroking Leo. Then they all walked uneasily along the side of the farmhouse.

They met Nick head-on. He looked wild and yet frightened, as if he could burst into tears. His chest heaved in gulps of air. His voice broke as he shouted at Jacob.

"Don't say it's not your own fault. You had your chance!"

"What is it?" asked Jacob. "Tell me." He put out his hand. Nick bolted past.

Jacob called after him, but he leaped into the car. It jerked into reverse and then shot forwards, mashing the grass at the side of the Land Rover.

An anxious feeling came over Peter. "Jacob," he said. "Nick was in the house. He took something into the yard. He didn't have it when he left."

Jacob went on staring at the end of the drive where Nick had disappeared.

"The front door's open," said Ben.

"In that way then," Jacob said.

70

He didn't say how odd it was. He just shut the door after they got into the hall. He took a key from a hook on the wall and locked it. Nick must have had his own keys.

Jacob sighed. "Well, put the kettle on the Aga, shall we? See what biscuits there are in the tin."

He went first into the kitchen. They came up behind him and stopped short.

They all gaped at the desk. The deep side drawer was pulled out, empty. The pig-breeding records were flung across the desktop. Jacob's strongbox was gone!

"That was what Nick had!" gasped Peter. He'd watched him escape with Jacob's valuables and not done a thing.

"Was there much money in it?" asked Ben quietly.

"The money doesn't matter," said Jacob. "It's the papers . . ." He went to the desk and moved the record books and opened and closed the other drawers.

He dropped into his worn armchair, looking crushed.

"The paper Nick signed to show I bought his half of the farm is in there. I should have registered it. There's no other proof that the farm's all mine."

"Call the police!" cried Peter.

"No, no. He's not himself. He's badly in debt, you see. Maybe he thinks this'll get me to borrow for him, but he knows I can't borrow the kind of money he's after. Perhaps he'll come back . . ."

Chapter 15

Peter crept up the side of the big barn with the flag. He knew
Ben was hiding somewhere in the farmyard, waiting to pounce.
He had to get over the gate to Dark Den.

He heard tyres scrunch on the drive. Jacob had gone to one
of the paddocks to fix some loose boards on the back of an arc.
They'd promised to bring Nick down if he came.

"OK, truce, truce!" Peter shouted. "Visitor!"

"Blast!" Ben stepped out from just inside the barn. He'd
been only two metres away, ready to spring. "I had
you!"

"Oh, *bad* luck, Benbo!"

As they came round the front, Ed Randall got out of his
Range Rover.

"Hello, lads. Jacob here?"

"In the fields."

Ed frowned at them. "Aren't you the boys who snooped
round my place and wrote that letter to the paper?"

Peter met his eyes. "I wrote it. We didn't snoop. You said
we could walk round."

"You looked too young to be animal rights nutters."

"We never thought about it before," said Peter, telling himself to keep cool. "We'd never seen animals kept like that before."

"That's modern farming. Saves a lot of time for staff. Not everyone enjoys dashing around outside in all weathers. Some land hasn't got good enough drainage for outdoor pigs anyway."

"Couldn't those farms be used for something else?"

"Listen, with so many mouths about, you can't take a sentimental attitude to cheap food production."

Ben suddenly joined in. "Most land can feed loads more people if they're vegetarian."

Peter shot him a sideways glance. Ben was really getting into this less meat thing. He'd tracked down decent-tasting vege-sausages now that even *he* didn't mind eating.

"Come on," said Ed, "you're not going to change the habits of people used to meat. They enjoy it!"

"I'm changing my habits," said Ben.

Ed laughed as a way of ending the conversation. "Jacob and I had better hope there aren't many like you then, hadn't we? Just show me where he is now, please."

Going through the farmyard, Ed looked up at Devil's Loft and the big barn.

"Buildings look sound." He had a smug expression Peter didn't like.

They took him down to a paddock where some sows were running with Jacob's boars. The sows stayed with the boars several weeks after mating. If any hadn't got pregnant, Jacob could tell because the boars would stand on their hind legs and mate with them again.

Tapping came from the bottom of the field where Jacob was repairing the arc. A partridge whirred up.

"Well I never. Are there many of those?" asked Ed.

"They like to scrape out nests in that rough corner," said Ben.

"Bit of fun for a gun then."

"Jacob doesn't shoot them," snapped Peter. "He says they're getting scarce round here."

He retracted the wire gate into the paddock. Leo bounded across, barking. He nosed around Ed and nudged his head into Ben, then Peter.

They'd saved the cores of apples they'd eaten earlier. They gave them to a couple of sows as they started down the paddock.

Other sows trotted over from where they were rooting in the shade of an oak. They sniffed hopefully. The two massive boars lumbered up.

"Hope they like strangers," said Ed with a grimace. He tucked his hands out of the way in his pockets.

To the animals, this promised further apples. Grunting, their mouths held a little open in the way of interested pigs, they pushed round Ed. Their heavy, eager bodies cut him off from Peter and Ben. A couple of them explored his trousers with their mobile snouts.

"Get off!" yelled Ed.

"They won't hurt you," called Ben.

But Ed's swagger disappeared. He hunched his shoulders and squeezed his legs together as if he were trying to make himself smaller.

"Get the ruddy things away! They're mobbing me!" He looked a real prat.

Peter could hardly believe it. Did he use protective boards

74

when he moved animals about? Hadn't he ever been with a herd of loose pigs before?

"He's probably afraid they're going to get even with him for what he's doing to the pigs at his place," he muttered to Ben.

Jacob saw what was happening and came up, gently swinging his arms.

"Hello there, Ed. Thought I heard you. Perhaps you'd like to come back to the house?" He moved between the pigs, patting one of the big boars. The animals stepped easily aside.

Once outside the paddock, Ed was soon perky again. He and Jacob walked up the hedgerow to the main gateway. The boys came behind with Leo. In the hedge, brambles were flowering where Peter and Ben would help themselves to juicy black-berries in September.

"Good stone barns in the farmyard," said Ed. "Ever thought of converting them into cottages? Make a nice little country development."

"They're working buildings."

"Ways of working can change. I expect you know why I've called."

"No."

"About your brother's debts. Having to sell his half of the farm to settle."

Jacob stared at Ed, but didn't speak.

"Hasn't he told you?" Ed looked a little embarrassed. "He's left me no choice. I've got to call in my loan."

He told Jacob that Nick had borrowed a huge amount of money from him two years ago, using his half of the farm as security. "Asked me to keep quiet about it. Didn't want to worry you since you rent the land."

"Rent the land?"

"I'd like to expand. I plan to pay the excess and buy his land outright. I know it's hard lines on you, and, unfortunately for me, your land comes between mine and Nick's. I particularly want that field below the wood. Why not come in with me?"

Peter listened in horror. So this was what that shyster had been up to. Dirty swindler!

"I'd like to have three or four new pig units up here," Ed went on. "Not near any dwellings, of course. You could stay on in the house and manage everything. Tail off this sort of thing." He gestured towards the paddocks.

Jacob opened the gate and held it while everyone went through. He clicked it together. Then he spoke quietly. "None of this is Nick's land. In so far as it's anybody's, and we're all only custodians, it's mine."

"I saw your father's will at the solicitor's in Whittlesford. The farm was split in half."

"Nick and I drew up an agreement of sale when I made the smallholding over to him to turn into the stables. I finished the necessary payments last November."

"You pay him monthly rent!"

"Not rent. It was part of the sale agreement."

"What agreement? It's not registered. Where is it?"

Peter and Ben looked at each other, aghast.

There was a second's silence before Jacob said, "It was stolen from the house yesterday."

"Come on, Jacob. Pull the other one. You're not serious."

"Quite serious."

"Were the police informed?"

"No."

76

"Why not? Who witnessed this sale deed anyway?"

"Dave Andrews while he was working for us."

"A dead witness! You really are having me on! That story's not going to hold much water."

Jacob didn't answer. Ed glanced at his face and saw it was completely straight.

"I hope we haven't got some unpleasant legal battle in front of us," he said. "Maybe you should think over my offer. I'm a good businessman, and you're a hard worker. We could make real money here."

They reached the yard. Jacob stopped walking.

"I'm afraid you've been misled. I'm truly sorry. But Ed, whatever the situation with the farm, I could never be part of raising animals in factory conditions."

Ed looked gobsmacked. "It's the solicitors then," he said abruptly. "Goodbye!"

He didn't wait to hear Jacob's goodbye. He scowled at Peter and Ben as if they had something to do with thwarting his plans and strode off. Leo followed a little way with his head low.

"He wants to build torture chambers *here*!" gasped Ben.

It was like a nightmare.

Peter kicked a stone hard across the yard. It whacked the door of the tractor shed.

"I wish the pigs *had* attacked him!" he shouted. "They can be locked out of sight in death cells while humans get the barns made into sweetie-pie cottages."

This was a proper farm. Everything was cared for—earth, plants, wildlife, animals. It *mustn't* become just a *business*!

Jacob looked back the way they'd come. The three of them got a picture of the other side of the wood where the plump

77

hedges and mature trees ended and the Randalls' featureless sheets of grain drifted away on both sides of the brook.

"We've got to stop him!" cried Ben.

"Get the police now!" urged Peter. "We all saw Nick."

Jacob shook his head. "It's a black day when you turn on your brother."

"But he's robbed you!"

"Even if we could prove that, I don't want him in more trouble."

Peter suddenly knew what they had to do. He seized Jacob's arm.

"We have to find the strongbox!"

Chapter 16

"It's no good," said Jacob. "I searched as soon as you went home yesterday, but Nick knows the farm as well as I do. The strongbox could be anywhere."

"He probably took out the important papers anyway," said Ben.

"It's a stout little box. I don't reckon he'd have had time to smash the lock." Jacob reached into his pocket and pulled out a key. "There's only one of these."

"He couldn't have sneaked back and fetched it in the night, could he?"

"Not with Leo sleeping in the porch. You know how he carries on when anyone comes. And I had the bedroom window open. To tell the truth, I didn't sleep a lot last night."

"Then it's here," said Peter. "All we have to do is look *everywhere*."

"You're good friends," said Jacob. "As soon as I get that arc shipshape, I'm going over to the stables. Nick and I have got to talk this out."

"And we'll start searching," said Ben. He smiled at Jacob. "Don't worry. We're going to find it!"

Jacob smiled back, but when he turned to go down to the

paddock, Peter saw that his thoughts were far away. Leo noticed too. He trotted beside him, looking up and bumping against his legs to try and get his attention.

"Did you see which way Nick headed when he left the house?" Ben asked.

Peter shook his head. If only he had. "We went to tell Jacob then." He whammed another stone across the farmyard.

"Never mind. He can't have gone far. It was only a couple of minutes before we met him coming out of the yard."

"But he was out of breath."

"How far do you think he could have got?"

"Not as far as the fields. Maybe the Peak."

Suddenly Peter remembered his foot plunging between the bales. A perfect place to stow something.

"Split up," he said. "I'll check out the Peak."

"I think it's in the Spook Room. It'd be easy to bury something in all that junk."

Ben suddenly realized that he didn't want to be in there on his own. "It'd be better to search it together though," he added quickly.

"No. We'll cover more places if we work separately."

Ben knew he was caught. He'd have to brave it. "I think I'll go home and get the big torch," he said.

Peter ran to the Peak. He began shoving his fist deep into every likely-looking crevice. He'd have liked to be mashing a fist into Nick's face for doing this to them. His hand got sore from the scratchy straw, but he kept punching.

After he did the top, he went round checking the sides by first leaning over from the edge and then standing on the ground.

When Jacob left to find Nick, Leo joined him. He wagged his tail and jumped about, hoping it was a game. Peter didn't pay any attention, so he sat down in sphinx position with his tongue hanging out and waited.

Peter sifted through the loose straw under the jump, then went to the other end of the stack and began to drag out the bales where they climbed up.

They were hard work. It would have been easier with two. But *he* wanted to be the one to find the strongbox. He *would* find it. He was good at finding things.

He yanked at the next bale. A stash of packed straw fell down heavily behind. Leo ran forward, growling. He nosed into the straw.

Peter rushed to pull him out of the way. As he swooped, two field mice popped out near his face. They skittered to the ground and zigzagged off. Leo ran after them yapping, but he hadn't a hope.

"DRAT!" Peter brought a fist down on the bale.

He was sure now that the strongbox wasn't in the stack. Perhaps the Spook Room *was* more likely. Ben could be up there finding it without him.

He went into the tractor shed and climbed through the trap-door. He could hear Ben shoving things about. He kept out of sight and crept round the wall to the doorway.

Stuff had been dragged out everywhere. The torch lay on a horse collar, sending a strong beam into the corner where Ben was going through some sacks. The rest of the room lurked in shadow.

Ben hated working with the torch propped behind him, but he needed both hands free. Everything outside the sharp light gave him the heebie-jeebs. Upright tools looked like people spying on him; the pile of harnesses looked like the ribs of a collapsed skeleton.

His own shadow kept turning up and moving beside him. Once it stuck its head through a coil of rope on the wall and turned into a hanged man.

He told himself to stop freaking out. They only called this the Spook Room for fun.

Suddenly, the torch flew up in the air by itself. A shadow leaped out of nowhere. It screeched, "AAAAAAAH!"

Ben backed away so fast he fell over.

Peter clicked the torch on and off, hooting.

"You stinker, Peter!"

"I'm a gh*ooo*lie!" Peter leaped over a wooden yoke and came at Ben with his hands above his head.

"Get lost!" shouted Ben. "Cripes, I almost had a heart attack."

"Got to keep your antennae out in the Spook Room. How you doing then, Benbo?"

"I've moved everything at least twice."

Peter flashed the torch over intersecting drag-paths through the floor dust. He could see that shifting this gear, like the bales, had been hard work without someone taking the other end.

There was no escaping it. If they wanted to find the strongbox fast, they should cooperate. He'd probably still be the one to spot it first.

He walked around the room with the torch. A lot of droppings splattered the floor. He darted the light upward.

"You had some company in here then, Benbo."

"What?" Ben looked up. Against a beam were a row of what looked like neatly folded purses.

"Bats!"

"Right on."

Ben was glad he hadn't known before. He moved well away. "Stop shining the torch! You'll wake them up!"

Peter laughed. "OK. Planning time. Next most likely place?"

"Didn't Jacob say Nick kept his first pony in Dark Den?"

"It's not going to be anywhere in the orchard. We'd have seen him from the drive."

"He had horses in the big barn before he moved."

"Sorted. Let's shoot."

"What about putting all this stuff back?"

"It'll have to wait."

The bar of the death slide was in place. Peter made his kamikaze run at it, starting up the bomber whine as he crossed the loft. He clamped a hand on the middle of the bar and leaped. His other arm swung loose, holding the torch.

The whine descended with him and exploded into crashing noises when his feet hit ground and pounded through the old swing frame. He ran back with the pulley trailer-rope to put the bar in position for Ben.

Ben steadied himself with a glance down at the frame and jumped. He always used two hands.

"Cripes, I'm knacked already," he said as he hauled the pulley into place again.

"Lightweight! Stop whingeing."

"Don't worry. I'm not stopping till we find it!"

Peter gave him the torch to shine while he hunted through the cupboards and shelves in the old tack room. Then they went on through the barn looking round the ploughs and harrow and inside the seed drill.

In the grain store, they swam their arms through the mound of barley left on one side and the mound of wheat on the other. The great slopes they slid down after harvest were thankfully gone.

They went on to the poultry house by the bottom of the orchard and looked under the straw in the nesting boxes.

"I know! Shift the woodpile," said Peter. "Could be in the cracks."

Ben followed him back to the top of the farmyard, feeling ready to drop.

Chapter 17

Leo trotted round the side of the farmhouse, bringing Mum. She put down a bag. Leo immediately sat by it and swept the yard with his tail.

"Is that nosh?" asked Ben. "You've saved my life!"

He let go the log he and Peter were about to move.

"No luck yet?" asked Mum.

"Don't worry, we're narrowing it down."

Mum had gone ballistic last night when she heard that Nick had stolen Jacob's papers. Ben told her about Ed Randall when he went to get the torch.

She grabbed the log Ben had dropped. "It's despicable! I wish I'd witnessed that agreement instead of poor Dave Andrews."

She jerked the log out of the stack. Other logs began to roll and bump down.

"Watch out!" yelled Peter. He jumped sideways, clinging on to his end of the log. "You want to give me flat feet?"

"Imagine that villain trying to cheat his own brother!" Mum ranted on. "He's always played hard up with Jacob. Plenty of money for cars though. For restaurants. For racing. Spend, spend like there was no tomorrow!"

They dumped the log. She gave it an angry shove with her foot.

Peter thought of himself kicking the stones across the yard. She flares up easily like me, he thought. Or I flare up like her. Ben doesn't lose his temper like that.

Ben's not as like her as I am. He suddenly wondered if it was more difficult for him and Mum to get on because they were alike.

They grasped another log.

"These are mammoths!" said Mum.

"I can manage." Peter tried to take most of the weight as they heaved. More of the pile tumbled away. He could see nothing was hidden among the rest.

"Aren't they that sycamore that came down in the storm last winter? Dad was going to cut them up smaller for the Aga."

She mentioned Dad matter-of-factly. You'd never guess she'd sat holding his picture and crying. She had an inside life she never showed.

"I love these rolls," said Ben, rummaging through the grub. "Oh, and I love those red pears. Chocolate biscuits!"

"Don't maul it all then." Peter went and seized the bag. "Sit on the logs."

Leo followed them over and plonked down again, drooling. He tilted his head with a tiny whine and gave them the soft eyes treatment.

"Don't even think biscuit, gobble-jaws," Peter told him.

He was famished, but his mind raced while he ate.

"Mum, would Nick really lie about owning half the farm? In court?"

"He must be willing to, but I wouldn't put it past the blighter to think Jacob wouldn't take him to court if it came to it."

"But how could he bear to see the farm wrecked after growing up here?"

"This probably all started as a trick to borrow money for the stables, and then he couldn't pay his debts. He's obtained money by fraud. That's serious. He's out to save his own skin."

"Have you come to help?"

"Too right. Where should I look?"

"We haven't done the tractor shed. There's all those paint tins and oil drums and clobber."

"I'll start there then." She went down the farmyard.

Peter tossed a piece of roll. Leo snapped it out of the air.

"Come on, hurry!" He stuffed a pear and half the biscuits in his pocket. "I'm taking mine with me."

Leo followed him into the welding shed, hoping for more scraps, but when Peter trod on a piece of corrugated iron, he skedaddled fast. He couldn't bear the metallic rumble.

Peter searched the workbench and the welding gear while he finished eating. Then he moved all the smaller stuff Jacob used to make the arcs.

He stuck his head into the farmyard and saw Ben lying against a log.

"Stop lunching it!" he shouted.

He ran over. Ben opened his eyes with a start.

"You skiver!" Peter yelled. "Thought you weren't stopping till we found it. Fat lot you care. Leave me to bust a gut while you mong out like a daytime hedgehog."

"I didn't mean to."

"Get your butt up here!"

"I'm coming." Ben staggered to his feet and hurried into the shed.

They moved all the big planks and pieces of metal, but found nothing. They went down to the tractor shed.

Mum wiped a grubby arm across her face when she saw them. "It's not in here."

Peter had a nose round himself. It was taking much longer than he'd expected. Somehow they were on the wrong track. It shouldn't be this difficult.

They walked back towards the porch, trying to imagine Nick's route. Ben looked along the ground.

"The drain!" he yelled.

Peter ran to get there first. He pried up the rim of the cover.

They all crouched around the hole. Thick sludgy water stood in the pipe below.

"Right, you going to stir the poopers, Benbo?" asked Peter.

"No he isn't," said Mum. "Get a stick."

Peter found one by the woodpile and prodded the pipe bottom. Then he poked sideways underground.

"Soft goods only. I could bend some wire and feel further along."

"No, I think Nick would've put it somewhere he could get at it quickly. He wouldn't want it to turn up later because someone was digging out a block."

Peter hauled the lid back in place.

Ben sat on his haunches and sighed. "This isn't so easy."

"Oh, *sharp*!" taunted Peter. It made him feel worse to see Ben getting discouraged.

They heard the gravel scrunch. Here was Jacob back, and they'd got absolutely nowhere.

"Let's just hope that rotter's conscience has woken up," said Mum.

Jacob met them with a crumpled smile.

"You're good to come over, my dear," he said to Mum. "I'm afraid I haven't seen Nick. He told Pam he was going away for a while. Left her and the stable girl to look after things."

"Does she know where he's staying?"

"No, she's in a terrible state." He shook his head. "I blame myself. I should have guessed he was desperate when he asked me to take a bank loan and lend him the money."

"You've been too generous all his life. Growing up means taking responsibility for what you do."

"*I* was irresponsible not to have that deed of sale registered. Left temptation in his way. He's never been a good manager, but I can't think how he's run up such an amount. Perhaps he got so beside himself, he thought he could clear his debts by betting."

"Jacob, was there a paper making the smallholding over to Nick?"

"Yes, he's got it."

"So, he's probably already borrowed up to the hilt on the stables. He might even be planning to use what's left over from selling half the farm to pay that debt. You've got to stop him."

"How can I?"

"A good lawyer would be a start."

Jacob hardly seemed to hear. He looked sick with worry. "I just hope he's all right. I wish I could find him. I'm going to phone round and see if anybody knows where he is."

He went into the kitchen.

Peter saw Mum had been right. Jacob would never fight Nick in court. His heart wouldn't be in it.

He clenched his fists. They had to find the proof. They had to stop Nick pulling Jacob under with him.

"Back on the case, Ben!"

Mum helped them search the buildings further from the yard.

They went round the outsides too. They moved coiled wire, stones, roof slates and timber. They prodded beanpoles through patches of stingers and wild flowers. They lifted fern fronds and shrub branches.

The sky clouded over. Greyness started to fill the spaces between things. They worked on, but hopelessness grew in each of them.

They ended overlooking the gate to the home field, much farther away than Nick could have possibly come. The swallows were gliding low in the valley. Jacob said it was a sign of rain when they caught their insects near the earth.

They saw him in one of the paddocks now. He walked in his steady, rhythmic way, emptying a bucket of feed in a long line with the pigs trotting after him. They imagined the ache he was feeling inside.

"I think we'll have to call it a day," said Mum sadly.

She stood between Peter and Ben with an arm resting on each of their shoulders, absolutely equally.

Chapter 18

Peter couldn't sleep. In the bottom bunk, Ben crashed out straight away. It made Peter feel lonely. He tossed from one side to the other. Thunder rumbled in the distance, as if in sympathy.

In his mind he went round the farm, ticking off all the places they'd searched.

If I wanted to hide something, he thought, and I were Nick ... But he didn't like imagining himself as Nick. He'd rather imagine himself as Jacob. Thank goodness there were people like Jacob in the world or you'd want to give up.

And Nick knew how brill Jacob was. He was his brother, for cripes' sake. Deep down, it had to be burning him up to treat Jacob like this.

He pictured Nick's screwed-up face when he came round the side of the farmhouse after stealing the strongbox. Running away from facing what he was doing to Jacob. Running, running, badly out of breath.

But Nick was a rider. He was fit. Peter only got that out of breath when they raced to the ceiling and back on the gym wall bars.

That was it!

How could he have been so thick?

Peter flung back the duvet. He dropped down on to the rug.

"Ben!"

Not a flicker.

"Ben! Wake up! I've got it! I've got it!"

"Whaaa?" Ben rolled over heavily.

"I know where the strongbox is."

Ben snapped awake. "Where?"

"A place just the right size, completely hidden, that we've used, and I bet Nick used when he was a boy."

Ben sat up. His mind raced to get there.

"In Devil's Loft, but not in the Spook Room," said Peter.

He saw it hit him.

"Cripes, it has to be! In the straw store. Behind the loose stones at the top of the wall. But how'd he get up there without the straw?"

"Used our tea chests. Stacked them."

"Yes!"

"Let's go and see."

"What, now?"

"We can easy sneak out."

"Wicked!" Ben fished under his bunk. "I've still got the torch."

They pulled on jeans and sweatshirts. Peter pounced on the torch.

They crept past Mum's room to the top of the stairs. The second and third steps always creaked, but they knew how to miss them. They grabbed the handrails on each side and hoisted themselves over.

At the bottom, they pushed bare feet into their trainers. Peter turned the key in the back door. In a moment, they were outside.

"I won't switch the torch on till we get there," he whispered. "Someone might see."

The night was muggy and dark. Thunder crackled closer now. As they crossed the lawn, the wall loomed blackly in front of them. An owl hooted, perhaps one of the ones that had nested in the big barn this year.

"Let's wake Jacob," said Ben.

"Not till we know for sure. 'Course, Leo might wake him when he hears us."

But when they climbed up the wall, there was no sign of Leo. Ben gave a short low whistle.

He didn't come. Ben wished he'd hurry up.

Suddenly, without warning, the farm flashed before them in a strange second of faraway lightning. It appeared like a mirage or a vision in a book of fairy tales, transported whole from somewhere else. And when the darkness returned, they both had a feeling like homesickness, knowing that their safe and magic place could really disappear just like that.

For a moment they waited, too dazed to move. Then thunder clapped.

"Come on," said Peter. "Let's shift!"

They landed one beside the other and ran. The long grass which they tore through without thinking in the daytime now seemed an unfamiliar barrier, tickling their hands, swishing round their legs.

"Listen," said Ben, slowing down. They heard muffled barking. "Leo!"

"Jacob must have shut him in the porch because of the thunder," said Peter.

"Blast!" Ben had counted on Leo being with them. The night began to feel scary. "Do you think we could let him out?"

"'Course not. He'd get too frightened."

They crept round the farmhouse, keeping their feet silent on the grass, and then tiptoed into the farmyard. It lay eerily still.

Ben moved closer to Peter. He wished he were in control of the torch.

Peter suddenly stopped and looked towards the orchard.

"What?" whispered Ben.

"Don't know. Something by Dark Den. The stable door creaked. Probably a fox."

Ben didn't like it. "I think we should get Jacob."

"Ba-by! Hurry, it's going to rain. I just felt a plop on my nost."

Leo gave a gruff bark inside the porch. Then he started whining.

"He's heard us," whispered Ben. "He wants out." Jacob might hear him, but he'd think he was complaining about the thunder.

At the bottom of the steps to Devil's Loft, Ben stood aside to let Peter go first. He thought of rats slinking across the floor above, of spooks leaping up from nowhere.

"That could have been a tramp in Dark Den. There could be a tramp sleeping up here."

"Don't be a nerd."

"There could!"

Climbing steps without a handrail in the dark felt really dicey, as if there were bound not to be enough room between you and the edge. Ben kept well against the wall as he went.

At the top, Peter pushed open the door and clicked on the torch. He tried to shine it across the Loft. It gave hardly any light.

"The battery's run down! You must have left it on, you *dim*wit."

"I didn't. It was on a long time this morning."

"Just what we need. Quick, move the tea chests before it snuffs it."

The door began to swing closed behind Ben when something swooped fast towards him. It flapped over his head and whooshed out into the night.

Peter stiffened. "A bat!"

Chapter 19

"Cripes, all the bats will be awake in the Spook Room!" gasped Ben.

"They'll be out hunting," said Peter.

"That one wasn't!"

"They're not going to collide with you unless they want to. Jacob says they've got better sonic detection systems than submarines."

Peter looked down and saw the torch reduce itself to a beady eye.

"This is useless!" He plonked it on the floor. "Twit! Imagine not noticing the battery was going."

"*You* could have tested it before we left the house."

Ben turned to find the one window next to the door. Its murky square gave enough light to show the open mouth of the Spook Room. Another bat might zing out any minute.

Peter dragged a tea chest towards the back wall. "Bring another one," he ordered.

"I can't see."

"Then feel for it, beanbrain!"

Ben groped the floorboards, afraid he was going to touch some lurgy. His funny bone caught the edge of a chest.

"Ow!"

"What now?"

"Whacked myself."

"You're *pathetic*!"

Peter had the advantage of facing the window and could see Ben's outline. He came back and yanked the second tea chest to the wall. Ben followed the noise with the third.

"Now we've got to stack them," said Peter. He got his bearings from the position of the window. "I think this is about right."

The first chest lay on its side. They bumped about with another one till they got it on top and matched them. As they heaved up the third, there was a flash of light, and thunder crashed overhead.

Then everything went mad outside. Rain drummed down as if it were trying to split the roof slates. In the porch, Leo howled, but his misery disappeared into the din.

"Gees!" gasped Ben. "We'll have to stay up here till this is over now."

"Who cares as long as we find the strongbox?"

Peter felt the edges of the chests and pushed the top ones just slightly skew to make foot ledges. "Give me your shoulder. I'm going up."

Getting on to the ledge of the first chest was easy, but when he let go of Ben's shoulder and went higher, the stack shifted. Ben felt it go. He leaned forward on his hands, making his body into a prop.

"Keep like that," Peter shouted down to him.

He crawled on to the top chest. The centre sagged. The plywood seemed a bit splintered.

97

He teetered to stand-up position. He'd never realized how much you depended on seeing things to get your balance. The rain hammering above his head made him feel even more woozy.

His hands walked up the rough surface of the wall. He clawed at the top row of stones. They were all dead firm.

He shuffled to the other side of the tea chest, getting impatient. He was probably going to have to get down and move everything again. He dug into each end of the next stone he touched.

Immediately, it swung out. His arms flew back over his body.

"Ca-ripes!" he yelled. He only just managed to keep hold of the stone and regain his balance.

He eased himself to a squat. "You were lucky then, Benbo," he said when he was close enough for Ben to hear. "You almost had your brain tested. Here, take this."

As he waited for Ben to feel for the stone and put it on the floor, he saw the tiny eye of the torch go out across the loft.

"Do you think anything's there?" asked Ben.

"Hang on. I've got to get the other one out." He tried to sound calm, but his heart started pounding harder than the rain. It had to be here. Had to be. Had to be.

He brought down the second invisible stone. He felt the tea chest give as he turned around. He moved on to his knees to hand the stone to Ben.

"Quick, this wood's dodgy!"

When he got back up, he spread his legs, trying to distribute his weight. It was awkward because he had to stand on tiptoe now.

His finger pads found the ledge where the stones had come away and crept inwards. The pounding inside him beat out into the dark. Had to be, had to be!

Had to—! He touched something cold and smooth. His fingers slid over a hard surface and around the corners of a movable object.

"Is it there?" shouted Ben.

Peter's hand reached the top of the object and found a looped metal handle. Then he was sure.

"GOT IT!"

"Really?"

Peter edged the strongbox off the ledge and clutched it against him as he slid down into kneeling position. He rested it a moment on the chest.

Ben reached up and touched the metal.

"*Yes*! Brilliant! Fantastic! Give it me."

"No, I've got it." Peter looped his hand round the handle. He grabbed Ben's shoulder and sprang down. The plywood cracked as he went.

"Who cares if we get soaked? Let's go and bang on Jacob's door till he hears."

"Sound!" Ben bobbed up and down in the darkness. He headed for the window near the door.

Peter came after him. He hugged the box, imagining Jacob's big smile filling his face when he gave it to him.

It would come out how he'd realized where it must be, and Jacob would say, That's my boy, and Mum would say, I knew if anybody could find it you would, and she'd send a message straight away on the e-mail to Dad—

Ben grabbed Peter's arm.

"Look out the window! A torch! Someone's coming through the orchard!"

Chapter 20

"Perhaps it's Mum or Jacob looking for us," Ben said, but he knew it wasn't. They wouldn't be looking in the orchard.

"It's Nick," said Peter. "Don't you get it? This is a perfect time to fetch the strongbox. He knows Leo'll be shut up and that Jacob will think he's going hyper because of the thunder."

"That was him you heard! He was hiding in Dark Den!"

"He was probably hanging round waiting for the storm to break."

"Do you think he saw us?"

"Might not."

The light moved to the gate and then went out. Whoever it was didn't want to be seen from the farmhouse. He was coming into the farmyard.

"We could jam the door with that pitchfork."

"Berk! If he can't get in, he'll know someone's here for sure."

Ben looked at the horrible dark hole of the Spook Room. There was no choice.

"OK. Down the ladder and run for it."

"We'll have to be careful. If he sees us in the yard, he might catch us. I'm not risking the strongbox after all this."

They dashed to the Spook Room entrance.

"We'll shut the door," said Peter. "That'll put him off the scent."

The darkness was as thick as velvet when they went in. They felt as if they were going to be smothered.

They both planned to slam the door, rip through and escape, but they'd forgotten the morning's work. The junk Ben had pulled out blocked them immediately.

And not only that. Although they couldn't hear or see them, currents of clammy air told them that the bats were on the wing. They had come in out of the storm.

Desperately they tried to clear a pathway for the door. They scrabbled about on hands and knees. Nick could be on the steps by now.

Their heads bashed as they both dived at a heap of heavy iron chain. They didn't waste breath complaining. They shoved together until it slid out of the way.

They had to lift the old door to make the hinges work.

"Hurry! Hurry!" Peter hissed. He wrenched the latch in place to hold it shut.

They turned around. They could vaguely see the opening into the part of the loft over the tractor shed, but the obstacle course in front of them lay hidden in pitch-black.

They scrambled forwards, tripping and crashing into things everywhere. The bats wove above.

Peter thumped Ben's arm. "Have you got the torch?"

"What?" Water had begun to pour from the gutters like taps on full, making it even harder to hear.

"The torch! Have you got it?"

"No."

101

"Drat! Then it's still on the floor. It's a dead give-away. He's bound to come after us now."

In this ruckus, it was impossible to tell if Nick had reached the loft, but it would only be seconds, and seconds for him to find that the strongbox was gone.

Peter thought fast. "We'll have to split. I'm the best runner, so I'll have to be the one he chases. You hide with the strongbox."

"I'm not hiding in here! He'll come back and find me."

"No, you go down the death slide. It's the best chance of getting away."

"At night? You must be bananas!"

"You've done it a million times. Go and hide round the back of the Peak. I'll let him chase me down the ladder and then leg it for the house. Even if he catches me, he'll think you've got there already with the goods."

Peter climbed over a horse collar and then pitched forward when his leg tangled with a harness. He clawed it off and crawled through the doorway. Ben staggered after him, booting away a basket.

They looked back. A glint of light showed around the edge of the door to the straw store.

"He's coming!" gasped Peter, pushing their door closed. "Shut him in with the bats!"

He flicked up the metal handle of the strongbox and shoved it at Ben. He hated letting it go, but he knew Ben would be a hopeless decoy.

"Down the slide!"

"I can't!" Ben was terrified. How could he possibly jump in the dark with rain pounding down on top of him? He'd lose hold. He'd fall.

Peter hustled him across to the pulley and rubbed a sleeve over the wooden bar to dry it. He pushed the bar into Ben's hand.

"Go!"

Ben's legs went liquid. The heebies he'd felt the first time he'd jumped were nothing compared to this.

"I *can't!*"

"Are you going to let Jacob lose the farm? Are you going to be responsible for more torture units being built?"

Oh, help. Somewhere down there was the swing frame. All he had to do was hang on. Do it for Jacob. Do it for the pigs.

But he couldn't jump one-handed like Peter. He slid both thumbs through the strongbox handle and clutched it against the bar. He gulped his usual deep breath, gripped for dear life and leaped into the storm.

Peter had no time to watch how he got on.

He heard someone stumble against the Spook Room door, shout a swear word and fall heavily. Peter imagined the torchlight catching the pointed faces and stretched wings of the wheeling bats.

He raced to fling up the trapdoor to hide his body. It must look as if he had the strongbox. He stood on the top rung of the ladder, balancing the flap in front of him.

The door exploded open.

Peter was prepared for Nick, but the mass of fury that erupted out of the Spook Room was a true devil. A pitchfork glinted in front of a frenzied figure that leaped towards him. The spikes burned and shook in torch glare. Then sharp light dived and stabbed his eyes.

"There you are, you little swine!" Nick screeched. "Where is it? WHERE IS IT?"

He lunged across the floor. The pitchfork rose ready to skewer its victim.

The torch swept the Loft as he came. The beam swung to the top of the empty slide wire. Nick saw the pulley was gone.

He swerved to the loading bay and aimed the fierce light through a thousand streaks of pelting rain. He noticed something and leaned out.

"Your brother's got it!" he shrieked.

He charged towards Peter. "*Out of the way!*"

Peter flung himself back on to the Loft floor. The flap fell open. The pitchfork crashed beside it.

Nick vaulted into the hole. Devil and torch disappeared in a trice.

Peter's breath rushed out.

But where was Ben when Nick saw him? Had he landed safely? Even if he was on his feet and running, would he have time to hide with Nick travelling this fast?

Perhaps Ben didn't even know he'd been seen.

Peter jumped up. He threw himself down the ladder, taking most of his weight on his hands.

He tore through the tractor shed. As he ducked into the downpour, he saw Nick belting hell for leather out of the farmyard in the direction of the Peak.

The plan couldn't have gone more wrong. For an instant he wondered if he should make a dash for the house and get Jacob. But there wasn't time. Nick would catch Ben and get away with the strongbox by then.

Could the two of them wrestle Nick while he was lashing out like someone possessed?

Peter sprinted across the farmyard. Rain had filled the tractor ruts and made streams. It swamped the insides of his trainers.

He leaned against the poultry house and watched Nick tear along the side of the Peak, keeping just far enough out to avoid the ragged sheets of water falling from the metal roof. He knew where he was going.

Sure enough, as he rounded the back of the stack, Ben shot out the other side.

He was cradling the strongbox against him like some helpless baby. He slapped through the puddles, struggling to keep his balance. He slid into the orchard.

In a second, Nick was round the Peak and after him. He flew over the mud, skidding recklessly. Ben hadn't a chance of getting away.

Peter raced off again in pursuit. He careered into the orchard. The sound of the rain notched to ear-splitting volume as he came in range of it hitting the Bog.

He expected to find Ben being driven to the ground. Instead he saw Nick's harsh light scanning the trees and Nick prowling up the side of the pond.

Ben had disappeared!

Chapter 21

Peter tailed Nick, dodging from trunk to trunk. Lightning flashed. A firecracker of thunder went off above.

He knew it was dangerous to be out in a thunderstorm. If only he'd let Ben tell Jacob what they were doing. But he hadn't wanted to be shown up if his guess was wrong.

Nick reached Dark Den. He opened the upper stable door and shone the torch inside. Then he turned back and hesitated near the top of the Bog.

Peter flattened against a tree. Water ran down his neck. His sweatshirt clung to his skin, sodden and cold. He began to shiver.

Nick retraced his steps down the orchard, searchlighting each tree he passed. Now and then he swung the torch around in all directions.

Lightning slashed the sky above the big barn. A second of glaring day showed the Bog blurred by rain, the thicket weird behind it. And the same second gave away Ben.

Somehow he had managed to climb through the summer plants on the edge of the opposite bank. He crouched in the reeds, clinging to the overhanging alder tree. The strongbox was clamped between his knees and chest.

The light went out. Thunder cracked and ground on and on like a terrible breaking-up of rocks.

The torch beam darted along the dense growth of the far bank. Nick could see how difficult it would be to reach Ben. But nothing was going to stop him now.

He kicked off his shoes and waded angrily into the Bog. His feet sank in the squelchy bottom. With a growl of disgust, he chucked his torch back on the bank and threw himself into the water to swim across.

Ben was trapped. He couldn't travel along the bank faster than Nick could get to him.

The fallen torch was still shining. Peter rushed into its light to show Ben where he was. He raised his arms in catch position, praying Ben would be able to see them.

Ben understood at once. He hauled up and hooked a leg around the alder.

This was where he'd thrown from before. The strongbox wasn't heavy, but how did the flying power of metal compare to wood, and in the rain? If he missed, he'd be giving it away.

The Bog wasn't deep enough for a man to swim properly. Nick had to keep pulling sinking knees and feet out of the mud on the bottom. He had to wrestle pondweed. It wrapped round his legs and arms with surprising strength. He swore at Ben as he thrashed towards him.

Ben gave no sign he was about to throw until Nick was only a couple of metres away. Then he yelled at the top of his voice. "NOW!"

He hurled the strongbox across the water.

Peter was ready. He'd made up his mind to go in and dive

Nick for it if necessary. But the strongbox sped towards him and crashed on to the bank at his feet.

Ace, Benbo! He scooped it up and raced for the gate. He threw himself over without looking back, yelling for Jacob.

He burst into the porch. Leo leaped and barked and licked the water running off Peter's hands. Then he cocked his ears. He growled deep in his throat and shot out the door even though thunder rolled overhead.

Peter lay on the bell and kicked the door with one numb foot and then the other. Water dripped from his clothes and made a pool on the tiles.

The light went on. The bolt drew back, and the door opened. Peter collapsed into safe, wonderful Jacob.

"I've got it!" he gasped.

Jacob saw the strongbox. "Where——?" He took it in his hands, amazed.

"Devil's Loft. Loose stones. I thought they might have been like that when Nick played up there."

"You're a marvel! But you're soaked, my love. You're out in this awful storm." He put an arm round Peter to draw him into the farmhouse, but Peter gripped him.

"You have to come! Nick's here. He's been chasing Ben."

"What? Now? Where are they?" Jacob stepped into the porch, doing up the trousers he'd pulled over his pyjamas. He grabbed a torch from the high porch shelf.

They ran out into the deafening rain. Within seconds, it flattened Jacob's hair and soaked his pyjama top.

They found Leo snarling and throwing himself against the bars of the gate like a mad thing. When Jacob undid it, he charged through.

108

There was no sign of Nick's torchlight anywhere in the orchard. The pond was empty. Both banks were still and dark.

"He's gone!" Peter ran down to where the torch had been. Jacob came and shone his light around the pond.

Where was Ben? Peter turned to Jacob desperately.

"Check the lane," Jacob shouted. "He might have parked there." He ran to the gate which opened from the orchard on to the drive.

He was out of hearing before Peter could begin to explain that Ben had been on the other bank. There was no way Nick could have taken him up the drive.

After Nick saw he'd lost the strongbox, he must have attacked him the way he laid into Leo that day. Hurt him and gone off.

Perhaps he'd knocked him under the water. Perhaps Ben was under the water now.

An unbearable picture of Ben clicked into Peter's mind— eager, cheerful, forgiving.

He was rotten to him. He did get at him. How could he? Ben was brill. He wanted him back!

Tears joined the rain running down Peter's face. He felt gutted.

"BEN!" he yelled, willing the horror away.

He was about to plunge into the Bog when he noticed that Leo hadn't gone with Jacob either. He was at the top of the thicket, whining and barking, trying to burrow in.

Peter raced to him. He screamed as he ran. "*Ben, Ben, Ben!*"

He went on screaming, sick with fear at what he might find, as he pushed in where Leo was digging. He hardly felt the scratches and stings as he fought the brambles and the lash-back of branches.

And then, when he was completely entangled and unable to move and sobbing so that he could hardly breathe, an answer came from further in. He gulped and froze stock-still. Was it a voice?

"Peter?" the voice called. "Is he gone?"

"BEN! Are you all right?"

"I'm ripped to shreds. I had to dive in here to get away. Are you all right?"

"I'm ripped to shreds coming to find you!" Peter hoped the rain would hide the choking in his voice, and then he didn't care.

"Has Jacob got the strongbox?" Ben shouted.

Peter had completely forgotten about the strongbox.

"He's got it," he yelled.

Ben's voice soared over the storm. "*YES!*"

Epilogue

Send:

It's sorted. Jacob's had to let Ed Randall have the field below the wood so he won't do Nick for fraud.

Mum went berserk about Jacob losing land. Then she got her head in gear and realized he'd be shredded if his brother went to prison.

Nick's gone bust. He's working as a live-in trainer near the racecourse. He comes to see Jacob every Friday now. He actually said "Sorry about chasing you" to me + Ben.

We'll never have another Creep and Chase like that one! We better not. Ben couldn't hack it.

Now Ben + I + Christopher Cole + Ben's friends are all collecting signatures, the petition to ban farrowing crates is really taking off. We're sworn to keep at it till the last crate is smashed up for robot fodder.

Harvest was a scorcher. The grain store, Loft and Peak are packed to the roof. Jacob says to tell you he's counting on you for next year. Mum still can't believe the Crat's come good and given you a decent job.

Hey Dad, *one week* and Ben + I take you on at footers!
Love,
Peter